Also by Lorna Jennings

Since the tragic death of her husband Owen, Susannah has maintained a strong bond with her son Ben. He was only a child when his father drowned, but Susa (as she is known to her friends) found great support through life-long friend Ray, and, with much success managed to retrieve her career in the theatre. Susa had already suffered the loss of her older teenage brother Peter whom she adored in her early years. She relied on his protection from her alcoholic father who detested her, but why? Thankfully her parents split up, and Susa with her long-suffering mother Elsie, left Bob and the run down farm to live at her delightfully inspiring Aunt Martha's.

With Ben now happily married to Amy, along with their two children Charlie and Martha, life seems to be in a blissful place. Sadly, little does Susa know, as she pulls out of her sons driveway, the major car accident she is about to encounter would change her life forever. Susa is rushed to the hospital and goes into a coma. She experiences four supernatural time-travels back to her earlier years that exposes all the lies and betrayals she never knew while uncovering the truth of who she really is! But has all this come too late or will she embrace her newfound life?

ISBN 9781800947887

This book is dedicated to
my son, Ché.

I take this opportunity to thank
Laura and Diane
for taking me in out of the cold.

And sister, Anna
for introducing me to
beautiful Benbradagh.

Lorna x

One

Nestled neatly into the brae of the Benbradagh mountain close to the historical town of Dungiven in Northern Ireland, sat a quaint and characterful, white-washed cottage where Joey and Heather O'Donnell raised their three children, Ruthann, Esther and Mosey. It was a relaxed and tranquil place, where the family enjoyed many years waking up to the call of the cockerel and the humdrum of tractors chugging up and down the quiet country roads. However, soon Benbradagh's small community would witness visitors of a different kind, or squatters as Joey O'Donnell would say. It was the time of the Cold War when tensions were growing between the US and the Soviet Union, and with both sides owning huge nuclear arsenals, the world faced the real possibility of nuclear conflict. The US Navy erected its communications base on the summit of Benbradagh, providing support for its large fleet in the North Atlantic. This propelled the generally peaceful and subdued location into the spotlight of world attention. Now, instead of the sound of corncrakes, cows and cockerels, they awoke to the cacophony of military jeeps, lorries and helicopters, having quite a distressing impact on the locals who were told that the transmitters installed on the summit would provide them with new and better television stations. It didn't take them long to realise that this was certainly not the case and now they had become the focus of international interest.

It was the long hot summer of 1969, a time of change for the people in Northern Ireland with the beginning of "The Troubles" having a detrimental effect on towns and communities all over the province of Ulster. People from both Protestant and Catholic religions had become arful and politically irate with one another which led t civil unrest with many unnecessary deaths, and fan es continuously in mourning. Towns became oppressive w h controlled zones from the British army, and high-secur alerts were set-up for emergencies in shops, hotels and bar for anything that looked remotely suspicious. Bombs and shootings were normal, everyday news, adding to social segregation that altered people's way of living, including that of the O'Donnells.

Joey had been brought up in the Catholic faith but married Heather from a staunch Protestant family. Her father and brothers, all loyal members of the Orange Order, naturally disapproved of her choice of a male companion.

Heather covertly ran off with Joey and got married in Gretna Green, subsequently being disowned by her family accusing her of bringing shame on them for not marrying 'one of her own kind,' but the new Mr and Mrs O'Donnell were never going to allow Northern Ireland politics to dictate their future happiness, instead, their union flourished. Their marriage was based on love, friendship and mutual respect, even though Heather made it very clear from the start that their children would be brought up Protestants. This didn't bother Joey as he wasn't religious, just happy to oblige as long as he had Heather by his side.

Thus, in the late 1960s, they found themselves in perilous times as mixed marriages were seen as an act of betrayal. Aware of this, the O'Donnells knew they had to be vigilant, especially running the business at the back of the cottage. O'Donnell and Son, car mechanics had served the locals for quite a few years. They had an excellent reputation, and Joey was able to provide more than adequately for his family. He had just finished a smart extension to their cosy kitchen making it into a larger more modern living area, and they took great pride in inviting the neighbours round to view his bespoke cabinets and the large window above the kitchen sink that now had the most scenic view of Benbradagh. It gave Joey great satisfaction to see Heather so happy as this was something she had always dreamed of.

Just a little further up the road from the cottage was a cowgate that led into one of Uncle John's fields; Uncle John being Joey's younger brother. It was a place of serenity for their very beautiful but mischievous younger daughter, Esther, as she would often go there and sit on the gate when requiring peace and quiet from the hustle and bustle of family life. It was always her favourite place, gazing out over the wide-open expanse of the green fields, magnificent sky, and of course, beautiful Benbradagh, where all her cares would disperse. It was her own private haven. Even as a child, she would demand her mother escort her up to Uncle John's cowgate where she could sit and look up at the big mountain.

Esther was now twenty-one years old but still sitting on the cowgate, although today was a different day and she really felt something exciting was going to happen; maybe even she could give fate a helping hand. But little did she know that her life was about to change, and her world would never be the same again!

Joining her on that exclusive experience was best pal and confidante, Katrina. Katrina had long, red curly hair and a loud distinct laugh. She always stood out from all the other boring fuddy-duddy friends who made their way in and out of Esther's life. This friendship had lasted quite a few years, and they had built a sturdy trust with one another. Katrina always found Esther to be an intriguing, unconquerable enigma as every time she thought she'd got to know the real Esther, she would then burst out with something so mind-boggling it left the very academic Katrina gobsmacked, giving her college dropout pal front place position without her even noticing.

It was another beautiful hot summer day, and they sat on the cowgate, discussing the important topic of planning their future until they noticed Uncle John driving his new Land Rover into the yard of his very impressive white house, which overlooked Joey's humble but characterful abode on the other side off the road. They waved at him, and he beeped the horn and disappeared into the garage.

"Poor Uncle John. Still pining for Aunt Brenda and pretending he's not. Moping about in that big house like he hasn't a shilling. Only for Stephen, he would be on his own you know."

They gossiped and laughed about whether or not Aunt Brenda had lots of secret lovers, or if Uncle John had problems of a physical nature, then a loud voice called, "Esther!"

Esther held her floppy hat with one hand and with the other lowered her dark sunglasses that reflected the tall, handsome blue-eyed Stephen, eagerly making his way towards the two ladies who at this moment were giving him all the attention he desired.

"He must be working down in Uncle John's back field today. Why doesn't he just stay there?" groaned Esther.

"WHAT!" Katrina laughed sarcastically. "You're sitting there looking like a Hollywood movie star, telling me you don't want him, huh?"

"Hollywood movie star, really?" replied a rather smug Esther.

A breathless Stephen eventually arrived at his destination, Esther's feet and managed to enquire boldly, "Would you both like to go into Dungiven later for something to eat or a beer, or something? I'll be finished in about half an hour!"

"No!" Esther replied quickly.

Katrina glared at her aghast. "Well, I'm not sitting here all evening. My bum's getting sore on this gate! So why not?" Esther's rudeness along with the heat had got Katrina irritated.

"Because I can't. I've something to do!"

"What?" shouted Katrina as she jumped down from the gate, looking rather confused by Esther's reaction.

"I'll tell you after, Katrina," she said and set her sunglasses back into place, turning her head away from Stephen.

"Okay, I get it," said Stephen feeling slightly punctured but familiar with Esther's mood swings. "Just tell me this, is your dad in? I need to see him."

"What do you want Dad for?" she snapped.

"I need to give him back the axe I borrowed from him!" He hesitated and then looked back at her crossly. "Anyway, why are you talking to me like that?"

Esther jumped down from the gate catching the hem of her blouse on a loose nail. "Awe, look what you made me do!"

Stephen and Katrina watched as she dramatized this scenario with sounds of frustration, ending the show by biting a piece of thread from her new cheesecloth top. "We only got this in the boutique this week."

Esther worked in the boutique in town and was privy to all the innovative fashions that enticed even ladies from the city to shop in Dungiven. The owner of the boutique encouraged Esther to wear some of his new garments, knowing her perfect physique was a first-class advertisement for his chosen masterpieces. He knew that Esther had an excellent sales-pitch and profits had elevated since she came on board.

"I'm sorry, ok! It's just I told Dad we went to the beach together last Saturday and I know he'll ask you about it. So, tell him we did, alright?"

Stephen looked shocked. "I don't think I'll be telling Mr O'Donnell lies like that now!" His voice shook with anger.

"Ack, Stephen, I'm not asking you to break the law! Sure, maybe me and you could trot over to…"

Stephen cut in sharply, appalled by what he was hearing. "TROT Esther O'Donnell? You're already a wild horse I can't harness. Trot on yourself!" and he stormed off, leaving Esther gobsmacked and Katrina's wide-eyed shocked expression turned into an outburst of laughter.

"Well did you ever?" declared Esther. "What's got into him?"

"What do you think has got into him?" answered Katrina. "You're so rude to him all the time, he doesn't deserve you." Katrina was flustered by Esther's arrogance. She'd always had a soft spot for Stephen and could never understand why Esther constantly had her guard up with him.

Stephen had been living at John's for several years now. He had been brought up through the care system yet had the good fortune to be fostered by John and Brenda when he was a child. They promised him the safe place of their home once he turned age and out of care. Brenda sadly left John, finding her new husband very quickly in their very friendly accountant, but John kept his word, and Stephen went to live with him. It was an arrangement that worked very well for both parties as John wouldn't have coped without Stephen after Brenda's swift departure. John taught Stephen everything he knew, from farming to building and called him the son he never had, and in return, it was easy to see how much Stephen loved and respected John for all he had done for him, but Stephen especially enjoyed living in close proximity to Esther O'Donnell.

"He's more like a cousin, Katrina. I've known him since I was a child."

"But he's not your cousin, is he?" She paused looking puzzled. "So, where did you really go last Saturday when you told your dad you were at the beach with Stephen?"

Esther was undecided whether to tell Katrina about the incident in Londonderry when she was accompanying her hippie friend, Jonny, a Queens University student studying politics, to a Protestant parade. She didn't want to hurt her lovely Catholic friend, yet deep down she knew that Katrina would understand. So, she told her all about how the parade passed through the Catholic Bogside area and how rioting broke out between the residents and the marchers. The two ladies never found their friendship religiously challenging before, because their lives seemed much the same. The only difference was that Katrina attended an all-girls school with nuns as teachers, which

Esther found slightly disturbing but just put it down to a 'Catholic thing.'

Katrina listened intently to her intriguing story, fascinated by Esther's bravery. She had seen the rioting on the news and knew it was still going on. Esther went on to tell her about having to run for her life, losing Jonny in the crowd and jumping on a bus heading out of Derry, just in time.

"Is Jonny alright?" asked Katrina in a sincerely concerned manner yet totally engrossed.

"Yes, he came to see me at the boutique. His arm was all bruised where he was hit with a brick. He told me that Terence O'Neil is talking about making changes and it's not going to be good, but Jonny says he's going to fight to keep Northern Ireland British."

"Oh, my word! What did you say?" said Katrina even more engrossed.

"What did I say? Well, I just told him I wanted nothing to do with it all, that even though my mum brought us up Protestants, my dad and Uncle John are Catholics. He was shocked at that!"

They chattered on and Esther spied one of the U.S. Army naval jeeps winding its way down the mountain.

"Oh, why can't everyone just go to Mass and leave people alone?" replied Katrina, oblivious to the fact that Esther was working on a perfect idea to have some fun.

Esther allowed Katrina to chatter about the awful state the country was in while her mind was set on other things, like the jeep that was heading in their direction.

"But we'll always be friends," went on Katrina, thinking her friend was listening to her. "Even though I'm a wee fenion and you're an aul proddie!" And she laughed loudly in that funny way that always made Esther laugh, even when there was nothing else to laugh at. But Esther was still concentrating on the jeep, and Katrina's next sentence was all she needed to bring her plan into action.

"Why does my life always seem so boring in comparison to yours, Esther?" having no idea what was about to happen.

Esther replied with a smug grin, "So, you'd like your life to be more exciting then, eh?"

"Well, yes," she answered dubiously now spotting a touch of mischief in her friend's eye.

Esther watched and as the jeep got closer but still at a safe distance, she lifted her hands and pushed Katrina's shoulders. Katrina tried to hold her balance, but in astonishment and confusion fell backwards to the ground. Esther realised very quickly that she may have hurt her without meaning to. "Oh, Kat, I'm so sorry. I didn't mean to push you that hard!"

"What the hell! Have you lost your senses?" Katrina yelled trying to get over the shock of what had just happened, and at the same time trying to pull her skirt down as it had inappropriately crept up to her waist. Katrina wondered what that was all about, unaware that two corporals had jumped out of the jeep and zealously made their way over to the damsel in distress. Esther tried to hide the delight of her plan coming into play.

"Are you ladies okay?" Their American accents were enough to attract Katrina's attention. She lifted her hand to her forehead, shielding her eyes from the sun and found standing at her feet, a long, gangly-looking character in full uniform. She inspected him from his shoes right up to his head and noticed that bizarrely he had the same colour of hair as she had. "Are you hurt?"

"Oh, erm, no. I'm okay," she replied trying not to show her embarrassment.

"Good, then let me help you up."

You could almost hear the romantic music in the background as their eyes met, and he took her hands, helping her up, then pulling her close to him. An embarrassed Katrina shook the grit from her clothing so that she could distract him from their evident mutual affection, while he happily stood and watched.

"My name's Ralph. What's yours?"

"I'm Katrina. You're very kind. I've no idea what came over my very strange friend!"

Esther had become so engaged in what was happening, that she hadn't noticed Ralph's colleague until Ralph took a moment from ogling Katrina and introduced them. Donny was a short guy with brown hair and a constant grin, one of life's charmers but never really achieving his target, and unfortunately for him, today wasn't going to be any different. He walked confidently over to Esther leaving Ralph to get better acquainted with Katrina.

"Hi, I hope your friend's okay. Ralph and I are from Arkansas in the United States of America," he added, trying to impress the beauty before him.

Esther smiled politely, knowing he didn't stand a chance, as she quietly envied the two lovebirds on the other side of the road. "We work up there on the radar transmitters," he said, pointing up at the US naval communications base. "I'd love to chat, but we have the Commander waiting on us in the jeep and we need to be on our best behaviour, know what I mean?" and he winked his eye at her with boyish sureness.

She rolled her eyes in disappointment, inwardly yearning for him to go. She glanced over at the jeep to avoid eye contact with her newfound fan. The roof was rolled back as it was such a hot day, and there sitting in the back seat was the most handsome man she'd ever seen in her life, staring right at her. He was a dark-eyed, swarthy Omar Sheriff look-alike and made every part of her tingle. Donny tried very hard to draw her attention back to him but to no avail, so he gave up, becoming increasingly aware of what was happening between this beauty and the Commander. Submitting completely, he shouted to Ralph,

"Come on lover boy. We need to go!"

Ralph jumped into the driver's seat and steered over to Katrina who was standing on the opposite side of the road from Esther. They said their farewells while Esther basked in the Commander's attention, and discreetly demanding more, she confidently ripped off her floppy hat, shaking her long dark hair, knowing full well the reaction she would get. The performance didn't fail. Donny couldn't resist.

"Hey! What's your name gorgeous?"

Esther walked closer to the vehicle but stood right in front of the handsome Commander, and looking him straight in the eye, announced, "My name is Esther."

The Commander's eyes were firmly fixed on her, but Donny replied,

"There was a Queen called Esther," knowing very well he was out of the game.

"I know," replied Esther. "I was named after her!"

Esther could feel something strange but very real happening to her. It was like she knew him. There was something enchantingly interesting about him and even without words, in those few moments, he had the power to induce her to succumb to his masculine charm.

"Beautiful Esther," finished Donny. "I hope you find your King!"

Ralph put his foot heavily on the accelerator and raced on down the mountain. It didn't take a flinch out of the handsome stranger in the back of the jeep, he just relaxed his arm over the back seat still checking on his enthralling encounter. Neither of them moved until they were out of sight from one another.

"What just happened?" squealed a very excited Katrina. "I'm meeting Ralph for a date in Renny's on Tuesday night!" She waited for Esther's jovial reaction but there was none. Esther stood rigid at the side of the road staring into space. "Are you alright?" but there was silence. "What's happened to you?"

Esther turned to Katrina looking like she'd been hypnotised.

"What's happened to you, Esther?" repeated Katrina, becoming concerned.

"What did just happen? I've never felt like this before. Did you see him?" she murmured, wiping a tear from her eye.

"What's wrong with you? Did he say something bad to you? I'll get your dad!"

"No, Kat! I'm alright. Did you see him?" she repeated needing a reply.

Katrina looked bewildered. "Who Esther?"

"The Commander, Kat! He's the most gorgeous man I've ever seen, but I just seem to have this strange feeling in my gut." She held her hand on her stomach, but Katrina still didn't get it.

"Maybe we need to get you to a doctor?"

"Not like that, stupid! I can't explain it. Who is that man?"

Katrina hadn't noticed and didn't really care. She had met Ralph and that was enough excitement for one day. "I don't know, Esther, but I can ask Ralph when I'm on my date with him on Tuesday night. Oh, he's so tall and handsome and… ginger! Just like me! I can't wait!"

Then a familiar voice beckoned, "Esther!"

She looked around and saw Stephen standing out on the road with his hands on his hips.

"Do you think he saw what happened?" asked Katrina anxiously.

"I don't know, and I don't care. Come on Kat!"

They walked quickly towards the cottage and passed Stephen on the way. He looked angry. Esther broke the uncomfortable silence. "Oh, go away, Stephen! Just go away! It's my life! Go try harness another!"

Two

The next morning was a cheerful, happy Sunday in the O'Donnell's, and while Joey admired every element of the new kitchen, Heather stared in awe out of the grand window with the magnificent view. "It's like a big, beautiful picture, Joey. Benbradagh looks breath-taking this morning."

Joey put his arms around her waist, and together they contemplated the beauty of their natural surroundings they were now visually connected to. "How did we ever manage to bring up the youngsters in that tiny wee kitchen, and without these beautiful views Mrs O?"

He squeezed her tightly to him and she turned to him grinning, "We managed just fine. But this is so much better and now I can keep an eye on you and Mosey working as well."

Joey was a proud father and had the comforting knowledge that Mosey would keep the business running if anything ever happened to him. He had taught Mosey the tricks of the trade and Mosey thrived on it. There was nothing else he wanted to do, except become a mechanic like his father. Heather helped in the business by keeping the books and handling all the administration. The family meant everything to her, and she wanted to support them all in every way she could. Knowing they all had their own unique dreams and aspirations, she always encouraged them, not like the discouraging household she had been brought up in.

"You'd never think for a minute there was any trouble in this wee country of ours when you look at all that, would you now?" Joey remarked as he rested his chin on her shoulder, absorbing the glorious scenery. "There's not even a sign of a Yankee right now! Not even the sound of a bomb or a gun!"

"I know, Joey," replied Heather firmly, "but there's a lot going on that we can't see and we need to be careful. Some businesses have to pay protection money. It's an awful thought! Like the mafia." It irritated Heather just how laid-back Joey could be when it came to the troubles, especially when she gave up so much for him and for that very reason.

He could feel her annoyance, so he gave her a reassuring hug and kissed her. "We've done nothing wrong, Heather. We're taxpayers. Okay, we were born into different religions that's all. Big deal!"

This very personal moment was cut short by the sound of feet running down the stairs. It was Esther and Ruthann. They made their way loudly into the kitchen, to be greeted by Mum and Dad embracing. "Please stop the lovey-dovey stuff," Esther commented cynically, "you're much too old!"

Heather pulled away swiftly and opened the window calling Mosey to come in for his breakfast, then took two plates of fried bread and sausages out of the oven and set them on the table. Mosey stamped his feet before entering through the back door to the usual command, to take his boots and overalls off before walking on the clean floor. Always obedient, he took them off and went to the sink to wash his hands. Mosey was the youngest of the three, a well-built guy just like his dad. He even had the same dimple on his chin but always tried to hide it each winter by growing a beard to stop everyone from calling him cute. His quiet manner permitted Ruthann and Esther to do all the talking so that he could silently spectate in the background.

Heather picked his overalls up off the floor and put them in the wash basket. "Is anyone coming to church with me this morning?" she asked.

"I am, Mum. I have to or Mr Stewart won't marry us. I'm meeting Robin there anyway," replied Ruthann. Ruthann was a hairdresser in the town but also worked at Renny's pub at the weekend for extra money, so that both she and Robin could afford their own home when they got married in a few months.

"Are you going, Esther?" asked Heather, knowing full well the answer.

"No!"

"Why not?" asked Ruthann grudgingly. "You're my bridesmaid!" unamused by her casual attitude towards her big day.

"I know I am! But could we please just get through one day and NOT talk about your wedding?"

"I'm sure it will be a lot worse when you get married!" said Ruthann, irritated by her lack of interest. "The whole world will have to know about that day! Poor Stephen!"

Esther looked at her with such contempt that everyone felt the change in atmosphere, so Joey decided to get them all sitting down around the table, while he and Mosey tucked into their breakfasts. This was always a good time for Joey to ask his usual questions, like what's happening in the family, so he could be kept in the picture with everything that was going on, that was important to him. "I was talking to Stephen yesterday, Esther, and apparently you forgot to take him to the beach last Saturday. So, were where you?"

"The worm!" Esther muttered, seething. "I'm twenty-one now, Dad. You don't need to know my private life anymore, the way me and Ruthann don't need to know yours."

"Now, you could do a lot worse than Stephen McCarthy, that's for sure," he replied, taking the opportunity to give his unwanted opinion.

Esther ignored his remark, grabbed a slice of toast and buttered it with all force until Mosey dropped a bombshell, "I got that new exhaust fitted on Liam McBride's motor, Dad. He'll be collecting it in the morning."

"Okay," replied Joey with his mouth full of bread and sausage.

"Oh, and one of them jeeps is coming in the morning. It needs fixing; I think it's the gear box."

Joey quickly took a mouthful of tea to wash down the food so he could speak but nearly choked at the same time. "What jeeps are you talking about son?"

Everyone quietened down, very conscious of the voice Joey just used, especially with the solemn look on his face. It quickly dawned on Mosey what he had just said, and as he slowly set his knife and fork down, he cleared his throat nervously. "One of the Yankee jeeps, Dad. One of the men called earlier. I can fix it; it'll be no bother to me. He's dropping it off in the morning."

Esther could feel herself weaken at the thought of the handsome Commander looking for her, but Joey loathed the US having their naval base on the mountain. Regularly he talked about the transmitters being an eyesore and how the Yankees had no right racing up and down "our territory" and having no respect for the locals.

"So, when did we start fixing their jeeps, Mosey?"

Mosey said nothing, trying not to make a bad situation any worse. But Joey had a lot to say on the matter and the family were going to hear, whether they liked it or not. "They've got a bloody nerve asking us. Have they not got a mechanic of their own? I'll tell ya what I think, I think there's more going on up there than what we've been led to believe. There's talk of nuclear weapons being up there and I don't like the sound of that! They've even started to call the back road The American Road! Well, it's bloody well not! It's no wonder Benbradagh means thief's peak in Irish, 'cause that's what they are! A bundle of bloody thieves!"

Heather never liked Joey raising his voice in front of the children, or swearing, but the children were now adults with their own views, and she was interested to hear them. Now, instead of telling Joey to calm down like she used to, she observed them all, interested to see and hear how they'd react to their father's political perceptions.

Ruthann was the first to give her thoughts in response to her dad's outburst. "I don't mind them, Dad. Some of them were in Renny's last night but they were so loud, Rita had to ask them to quieten down. The girls were all loving it though because they were buying them drinks and chatting them up. Lizzy and Trish had smiles on them like Cheshire cats."

Esther sat quietly having many questions running through her head, yet knowing she had to be careful. Who was that in the jeep talking to Mosey? Was it the Commander? Was he in Renny's last night? He couldn't be interested in Lizzy and Trish because nobody is, they're just two busy bodies who try to get all the gossip because their own lives are so boring. However, she needed to know, and it was her time to enquire.

"They're only doing their job, Dad," she pointed out gently, eager for a reaction. Heather agreed with her and Joey seemed a bit calmer now that he'd got his frustration of Mosey's compliance to the Yankees out of his system, at least for the moment. That made it easier for Esther to now probe Mosey.

"It was probably just one of those young Corporals, anyway," she said, knowing one way or another there would be a reply. It worked.

"Oh no it wasn't," answered an unwavering Mosey who was just about to bite into his second sausage. "It was an older man, very official-looking, swarthy. He certainly wasn't a Corporal. He's definitely not somebody you'd see plodding around Dungiven that's for sure."

He laughed but Esther didn't, she knew it was the Commander, he had come looking for her, she just knew it. Frustrated she'd missed him, and blaming Ruthann's chatter about wedding dresses, she still had to know more without starting her dad off in a rage again.

"He sounds like he genuinely needs help. So, he'll be back in the morning then?"

Ruthann looked questioningly at her. Esther knew she was onto her but desperately needed Mosey to answer.

"Yes! Now let me finish my breakfast!" he answered wanting this uncomfortable conversation to end.

Esther looked at Ruthann, who was looking suspiciously right back at her waiting for her next question, but Joey got in first, "We're not that hard up for money that we need to take on their work!"

It was all discussed at full length and Joey allowed Mosey to fix the jeep as he'd promised but that was to be it. Mosey agreed and everybody was satisfied, apart from Esther.

"What time is he coming in the morning, Mosey?" she asked cautiously but Ruthann knew there was something fishy going on.

"What's all the questions for, Esther? Why are you interested in what time he's coming?"

Esther noticed her mum now looking at her too, so she tried to brush it off swiftly, "I'm not asking questions! I'm just having a conversation, and I'm not interested in anything or anybody! Okay?"

She got up from the table obviously agitated with Ruthann and headed up to her room, as Mosey shouted the necessary answer, "About nine-ish."

That was all the information she needed, now it was time to plan and prepare. It was exciting. She knew she'd see him again, maybe not at home though, but she didn't mind as long as she did see him.

Three

The next morning a perfectly groomed Esther made her way down the stairs and over to the kitchen window, followed by an inquisitive Ruthann who had discreetly observed her for the last hour preening herself as if she was going to appear in a Miss World contest. Ruthann was used to Esther's morning preparations and constantly waited patiently in line for the bathroom to become unoccupied because Esther always took her time, but this morning it was even longer. There was definitely a man involved, and she couldn't wait to see what was going to happen next. Esther had got more and more aggravated with Ruthann watching her every move. She really wanted her to go away.

"Why don't you just go to work Ruthann, instead of following me around like some sad old drivelling hound dog?"

Ruthann laughed, which irritated her even more, but she tried hard not to show it.

"Mrs Murphy cancelled her appointment this morning, so I don't have to be in until later. I didn't know I was bothering you?" she said sarcastically.

Esther was obviously angry but tried to make herself look busy by putting the kettle on and taking cups out of the cupboard. Ruthann sat down at the table and watched the show, knowing exactly what was going on.

"Are you not going to work this morning? Maybe something more important happening?" She sniggered.

Esther, unable to hold her fury in any longer roared, "Look here, Ruthann!"

Just then she heard the jeep drive into the yard, and she immediately scurried to the window. Ruthann couldn't keep the laughter in. "Is it Mr Wonderful?"

Ignoring Ruthann, Esther ran her fingers through her immaculately styled hair, then opened the back door walking as calmly and sophisticatedly as she possibly could out to the yard. But as she got closer to the jeep, she realised the driver wasn't Mr Wonderful, it was Donny! Esther was gutted. Donny bellowed Hello to her but she turned speedily and ran back into the house, through the kitchen and up the stairs, finally throwing herself on top of her bed. She sobbed, again pursued by a bewildered Ruthann who certainly didn't expect that reaction. Ruthann tiptoed into the bedroom finding her sister now in floods of tears.

"What's wrong with you?" she asked quietly with all sincerity realising this wasn't a show, or if it had been it wasn't now. She vigilantly crept over to her and sat on the edge of the bed, gently putting her hand on her arm.

"Go away!" Esther screeched. "You've had your laugh now! Just go away."

Esther's strange behaviour shocked Ruthann, she had never seen her sister in such a state before and truly wanted to help her. "I'm not laughing! Who was that guy out there? He knew you! Do you love him?"

Esther turned to her with tears running down her face. "No, I don't love him. That's Donny. I thought he was someone else. I really needed him to be somebody else!" There were more tears.

This was a revelation to Ruthann. She had no idea Esther had fallen in love. She could have any man she wanted, yet never seemed interested, apart from Stephen, and that was only because he was convenient for her.

"I never thought I'd see you cry over a man, Esther. Tell me who you wanted him to be, maybe I can help you?"

As sisters, they were fairly close, and Esther knew Ruthann wouldn't tell their parents, so she told her everything that had happened and how she felt, even though there wasn't really a lot to tell.

"Oh, I think I know the man you're talking about," said a deflated Ruthann, who thought she was going to hear about a handsome young corporal sweeping her off her feet, not a Commander who was old enough to be her father. It just didn't sound right to her.

Esther eagerly pulled herself up from the bed. "How do you know him? What's his name?"

"I don't know his name, but he stays at Renny's sometimes when he's up at Benbradagh. Rita gives him the good room. I also know he does a lot of business up at the Castle too. Rita says that Marianne Stellabrass has an eye for him."

That was great news! He wasn't in her imagination he was real, and she was going to see him again. But when?

"Is that the good-looking older woman? The woman whose husband died and left her a fortune?" she coyly asked.

It was, but it didn't matter to Esther who Marianne Stellabrass was, or how much money she had, the chemistry they had together that day was enough to reassure her there was more to come.

"I'm worried about you, Esther. You know there's no way Mum or Dad would ever agree to this. Especially Dad, he'll be furious. He's a Yankee and so much older than you; you don't even know if he has a wife and family back in America. It could never work, and what about Stephen? He adores you and would make a great husband, besides, that Commander, well, he's not like us."

But it didn't matter what Ruthann thought, Stephen never made her feel the way he had. Even if Ruthann's words were true, it still didn't make any difference, he just wouldn't leave her thoughts. She really wanted her sister to understand but she was the logical and practical one while Esther was now a hopeless romantic, even though she had never planned to be.

"I've got to see him again. I need him and I didn't know I needed anyone until I saw him that day. I know you don't understand, Ruthann. Nor do I! Oh, I wish I could love Stephen, it would make my life so much easier, but I don't!"

More tears rolled down Esther's face while Ruthann held her tightly and gave her own words of wisdom, "Well, Esther if that's the case, and I'm beginning to think it is, you had better get used to those tears, because there'll be a lot more of them before it's all over if he's the one you've chosen?"

She gently released her while getting up off the bed and made her way down the stairs leaving Esther to ponder. How can Ruthann think like that? It certainly wasn't the future she could see. She didn't choose him; it was like fate had taken control, that 'meant to be' thing! He would whisk her off her feet and she would become the dutiful wife of a well-respected Naval Commander, and they would go to banquets along with well-known dignitaries from far and wide and travel the world making love under moonlit skies. Mum and Dad would be so proud! How exciting!

Then bang – it was the front door and she could hear Heather shout,

"Why are you not at work Esther? Are you sick?"

Esther quickly exited her dreamworld and got up, grabbing a handful of tissues to dry her face and dashed down the stairs. "I'm going to work now. Were you over at Uncle John's?" she said, changing the subject subtly.

"Yes. He and Stephen are coming over for dinner this evening. Will you join us?"

"I'm not sure. I think I'm meeting Katrina."

Heather looked disappointed. She would do anything to get Esther and Stephen married, but it was getting predictable and exhausting for Esther, she had other plans… to find her Commander!

Esther spent all her spare time trying hard to be in the right place at the right time where she could accidently bump into him again. In Renny's, at the Castle and even sitting on the cow-gate hoping he would drive past, but he didn't. It was like he'd disappeared.

Days turned to weeks. She watched as Katrina's romance with Ralph flourished, how happy they were together, and how excited Ruthann was about the wedding, spending the rest of her life with the Resourceful Robin (as she called him) packing all her bits of furniture to bring to their new home in Limavady where Robin came from.

Esther found herself feeling so lonely that she even started going to the pictures with Stephen, much to Heather's delight, but it was just to kill time until he came back, assuming he was away. But it didn't matter, this man whoever he was, just wouldn't vacate her thoughts, and somewhere deep inside she knew she would see him again soon.

Four

It was a rainy evening in late September and Esther and her mum where due to have their hair styled, as a practice run for the wedding in the salon Ruthann worked in. The weather was getting worse, though, with the addition of thunder and lightning. The people of the town were concerned that there could be a power cut, so some shops closed up early, the salon was one of them and so was the boutique. Esther locked up the boutique to go and meet her mum at Renny's where Joey was going to collect them, when she heard a horn beep and turned to see Stephen in Uncle John's van. He shouted out to her,

"Hey! Do you need a lift, Esther?"

"No, it's okay," she yelled back loudly through the noise of the rain. "Dad's collecting me and Mum at Renny's."

Stephen drove off and Esther soon gave up on her long, black leather coat for protection as the rain was pelting down and she was soaked through. Running as fast as she could, she just managed to make it to Renny's before another clamour of thunder, so loud it sounded like the world was coming to an end.

"Oh, Esther!" hollered Rita, hurtling out from behind the bar and fussing about trying to take the drenched coat off her and hanging it on one of the coat-hangers at the doorway. "Go on through to the big fire Tommy lit earlier. Sure, it would dry the Atlantic the flames are that high! Your mummy's just away down to Eileen at the Mace to get a few groceries. She told me to tell you she won't be long. Sure the weather's shocking. I hope it's not like that at Ruthann's wedding. Me and Tommy are looking forward to it."

Rita was still talking as she disappeared out the back, so Esther made her way through the empty lounge to the two Queen Anne chairs placed in front of the large, raging fire. As she headed to the one facing the doorway, she could smell a beautiful aroma of expensive aftershave lingering in the air, but it wasn't until she sat down, feeling like a drowned rat and having a loud sneeze, that she noticed she wasn't on her own. Before she could see who it was, a white folded handkerchief was placed in her hand as she sneezed again, then managing to look up, her heart missed a beat, there he was! Sitting directly in the chair opposite was the Commander looking so handsome and well-groomed. He smiled at her while she tried desperately to wipe the water drips from her face and hair, hoping that her eyes weren't all smudged with wet mascara. Oh, no! How could this happen today of all days? But she gave up panicking once his dark eyes told her it didn't matter.

There was a quiet moment as she relaxed, and they stared at one another until he said in his deep, masculine voice, "It's nice to see you, Esther. I knew we would meet again." She wanted to speak but nothing came out because of shock and nerves. He observed this and politely spoke to hide her embarrassment, "May I introduce myself?"

This was it, the moment she had waited for, longed for. If only he knew how much she had thought of him, even crying over him yet ironically, she didn't even know his name. Here was the man who had turned her life completely upside-down without saying a word, now directly in front of her about to disclose this valuable piece of information.

"Yes, please do," she managed to say while sneezing again. He waited graciously.

"My name is Rueben. Many know me as Commander Redpath but only a few I allow to call me Rueben. You of course may call me Rueben."

What a beautiful name, she thought, like a movie star, Rueben Redpath. He had such a respectful way with him that made her feel at ease. In his hand was one of Rita's finest brandy glasses and she watched while he sipped slowly, savouring every moment while his eyes fixed on hers. She could hear alarms in her head cry out to be careful, but she ignored them, content to have no control.

"Did you go to my house, Rueben Redpath?"

Rueben was fascinated by her, and she knew it, but she was equally captivated by him. This was definitely meant to be, and as he spoke, she was directed to every small laughter line that gathered so neatly at the side of his deep dark eyes, his thick eyebrows and seamlessly groomed moustache matched his shiny black hair that was smoothly combed back, complimenting his distinguished face.

"Yes, I did. I had to. I needed to see you again. You are a very beautiful woman, and I can't keep my eyes off you! You feel it too don't you, the heat?"

She could feel it alright. She could also feel herself getting emotional knowing nothing was ever going to be the same again after this liaison. Commander Redpath had authority, not just over his army, but over her too and she was more than willing to obey his orders.

"I feel the heat from the fire," she smiled. "Maybe not the fire," she paused, "maybe you."

Again, their eyes connected. She could see he liked her reply and gave her a smile showing his whiter-than-white teeth. "You're used to people telling you how beautiful you are, are you not?"

She was, but right now he was the beautiful one while she just dripped. Knowing there was so little time, she still needed to find out some more about him, and with his natural swarthy skin along with his distinctive accent, she awkwardly asked him, "Where are you from?"

He took another sip of his brandy and then gave a little laugh. "I'm an American citizen but with a touch of Eastern promise."

She wondered what that meant but now wasn't the time to ask. There were lots of questions running through her mind, but she felt silenced, consequently allowing him to lead these precious moments.

"I'm staying here, Esther O'Donnell." It seemed unquestionable and comfortable that he knew her name, pleased that he had undoubtably gone out of his way to find out who she was. "I have a superbly comfortable bedroom."

"You do?" she replied, blushing. Surprised by her own reaction knowing only too well that if any other man was so bold as to say that to her, she would tell them bluntly where to go, but on this occasion, she wanted him to take her by the hand and lead her to his superbly comfortable bedroom where they could be alone, and no-one could interrupt.

"Let me get you a brandy. It will warm you up on the inside, while the heat," he paused, "from the fire, will dry you on the outside."

"I'd like that," she replied, her heart racing again.

But right at that very moment, the door banged open, and Heather made a big entrance with her umbrella and groceries, shouting about how awful the weather was, having no idea that her daughter was being unashamedly seduced a few yards from her. Rita appeared and they chattered on about the weather and the wedding, and the world started up again, and with that, Esther rose to her feet, grateful that Heather and Rita were completely unaware of the tall, dark stranger's presence, never mind anything else. His warm, manly hand gently took hold of her arm, and she didn't flinch, for if she did, she knew it would distract her mother and that was the last thing she needed, nothing was to ruin that moment. He stroked her arm softly knowing exactly what was going on, they were on the same page, as he gently whispered,

"I'll see you soon, won't I?"

She nodded, so that he would know she was saying yes, while Rita thought she was just agreeing with her. He gradually let go of her, and Heather, in her high-pitched motherly voice cried out, "Come on Esther, your dad's out in the car waiting for us, we'd better go love!"

Esther grabbed her coat from the hanger and put it on, leaving as quickly as she could. Rita said goodbye and watched them go, but as she headed back towards the kitchen, she caught sight of Rueben setting his glass on the table where Esther had been. She looked confused but went on about her business.

Holding his handkerchief tightly in her hand, trying hard not to cry yet overcome with joy at having met Rueben Redpath, Esther now had to endure Joey announcing to them that a bomb had gone off in Belfast killing two people. That was going to make things difficult as Heather would now worry and want to know where she was all the time, but not even a bomb was going to dampen her spirits today! She had found her Commander and that was all that mattered.

The next day, Katrina told Esther that Ralph needed to speak with her. She met him and he informed her that Commander Redpath had to leave Benbradagh urgently, but he would be back in a few days. That was the confirmation Esther needed. She was now in his life and waiting for him would be worth it. A few weeks went by but there was still no sign of him. Esther clung to his handkerchief waiting as patiently as she could, absorbed in the thought of being together again.

Five

It was the day of Ruthann's wedding and there was such excitement in the O'Donnell household. Joey was in his element, sneaking into the pantry and pouring himself a bit of Dutch courage so that he could escort his beautiful daughter down the aisle. Mosey, at long last was out of his overalls and looking very dapper in his navy, three-piece suit and matching bow tie, but really not knowing what to do with himself. Up in Esther's room, Heather helped Ruthann with her veil while Esther quietly decided that her concern for Rueben's whereabouts was not going to stop her from enjoying this special day. The back door opened, and Uncle John arrived with Stephen just in the nick of time for a glass of Irish whiskey with the father of the bride.

"Uncle John, we need to get going soon!" whimpered a flustered Mosey, who was already feeling the pressure of having a day off from his beloved motors. As they knocked back the whiskey, Esther came running into the kitchen to get some pins out of the drawer. All dressed up in a pink satin bridesmaid dress and her hair up in a very classy beehive, Stephen couldn't take his eyes off her.

"Esther! You look beautiful."

"Thank you, Stephen. You don't look too bad yourself." And she ran back out leaving Stephen speechless.

"Right, come on now," yelled Mosey who was getting more agitated by the minute, standing about doing nothing. He ushered Uncle John and Stephen out to his car leaving Joey singing, "I'm getting married in the morning..."

Heather spied him pouring another whiskey as she came into the kitchen, all ready for the wedding.

"Joey O'Donnell! Now that's enough! This is Ruthann's big day and you're not going to ruin it for her."

He walked calmly over to her and pulled her into his arms. "I'll never let any of yous down, Mrs O!" he said and kissed her.

"Ack, you've aul whiskey breath, Joey." But as she went to walk away, he pulled her back.

"Heather O'Donnell, you're the most beautiful woman I've ever laid my eyes on! You're the only woman for me."

Heather laughed knowing how sentimental he was at weddings, but this was a very important one and it was time for him to do his duty. Esther and Ruthann came down the stairs giggling with anticipation and excitement.

Joey watched as the three of them laughed together in their wedding gowns and tears filled his eyes. "I'm the luckiest man alive!"

The wedding car arrived to take them to the Church of Ireland on Main Street, Dungiven. All the people from the town were there to see them enter the church single and leave as the new Mr and Mrs Harvey. Robin, who was a professional photographer had his colleague there taking the photographs, but Ruthann did have to remind him that he was the bridegroom and not the photographer today. The wedding party and special guests all walked the short distance together to Dungiven Castle where the wedding breakfast was to be served. There were just a few guests including the Reverend Stewart who performed the ceremony, Tommy and Rita from Renny's, Uncle John, Stephen, some of Robin's family and a couple who were close friends. After that, Tommy and Rita organised some music and a buffet for the wedding party and other guests in the evening at Renny's.

Tommy liked a wedding, and this one was no exception. Having one whiskey too many, he staggered over to the Reverend Stewart and announced in front of everyone, "Now, that was a lovely service Father, would you like a wee port?" as proud as punch.

Rita coughed loudly having just taken a small sip of her champagne, dreading to hear what he was going to say next. Everyone waited intently to hear Mr Stewart's reply, knowing the Reverend was not a partaker of any kind of alcoholic beverages.

"Now Tommy, what are you calling me Father for? I'm not a priest! I'm Reverend Stewart, a Protestant Church of Ireland minister! Surely in this day and age, you know the difference!"

Tommy looked at him very puzzled but replied in his confused drunken state, "Oh, I'm so very sorry Reverend Stewart. It's just that I'm not a very religious man you know. I only go to Mass when Rita makes me, and to be honest with you, well you all look and sound the same to me!"

The Reverend Stewart was not amused. "But we're not all the same Tommy! Although I can understand when you've consumed half a dozen whiskeys that you might think so!" And he laughed a big laugh easing the tension.

Tommy continued, "So that's a no to a wee Port then, Reverend father?"

Rita could take no more and marched around the table to him. You could see by the look on her face she was fuming, and the look on his was one of fear. She pulled him by the arm back to his seat and gave him a quick sharp slap on the back of the ear. "You aul eejit! Have you forgotten you're working tonight? No more drink for you, do you hear me!"

A very humble Tommy replied, "Yes, love."

The guests tried their best not to laugh, but Heather, Esther and Ruthann excused themselves from the table and rapidly made a quick exit to the powder room, unable to keep their hilarity in any longer. On the way up the corridor, as they laughed profusely about Tommy, Esther spied a door to one of the conference rooms slightly open, she walked a little closer curious to see what it was like inside but overheard a voice she recognised. Moving closer, she pushed the door further and her hopes were confirmed. Just a few yards from her stood Rueben with four other official-looking men. He was standing opposite them behind a large desk. Esther signalled to Ruthann to go on ahead and Esther stood at the door, her heart beating faster and faster. It only took a few seconds before Rueben felt her presence and looked up. Esther, now having the advantage of distracting him on her terms and feeling a lot more confident with her appearance than the last time, smiled at him. Immediately he stopped what he was doing and practically ran over to her, leaving the men mesmerised.

"Beautiful Esther!" He opened his arms wide and hugged her. At long last they were together again. She knew by the way he held her that he was undeniably worth the wait. "I haven't been able to stop thinking of you since we last met."

She pulled back and looked at him in shock. "But where have you been?"

"Work, my darling, is my life. That's why it's so good to see you."

"Won't those men want you back in there?" she asked yearning for his full attention.

"Those men take their orders from me! You're like my angel." He pushed her back, looking her up and down. "I hope it wasn't you that got married?"

"It's not my time yet!" and she laughed nervously.

He answered with a nice, yet strange reply, "He will be a very lucky man, Esther!" sinking his eyes into hers but it was her heart that sank. The voice within her wanted to say, 'Don't you want to be the lucky man? You're the one I want!' But instead, she blushed and agreed, "He will."

Once again, the world stood still, nothing or no one else mattered. He pulled her close to him and held her tight, whispering in her ear, "I'm staying at Renny's. Room Three."

She could feel that heat again! "We're all going back there for the party later," reassuring him she would be there.

Her heart now leapt with excitement, knowing at last they would be alone, but anxious because of what might happen. Esther had never been in that position before, not even with Stephen.

He squeezed her inappropriately closer to him and again whispered in her ear, "Will you dance with me, Esther?"

"I'd love to dance with you Rueben."

Just then a door squeaked, and the sound of footsteps came up the corridor. She pulled away and turned around to see Stephen walking towards her. He looked confused as to why she was standing there on her own, but as he got closer, he saw Rueben. His look of confusion turned to one of anger and he glared at Rueben, then back at Esther.

"They're getting ready to go, Esther. I thought you were with your mum and Ruthann?"

"We'll be there in a minute. I'm just waiting on them."

He walked away with his head down like someone had just kicked him.

Rueben gently turned her face to him. "He loves you. I can see it in his eyes. You're going to break his heart."

She touched his lips with her finger. "It shouldn't matter to you how he feels."

He kissed her finger and put her hands down to her side as the sound of Heather and Ruthann could be heard laughing, but again he reminded her, "I'll see you later at Renny's. Don't forget, upstairs, number three, the door with the heart on it!" and he made his way back to the men who had tried to give him his privacy, even though they enjoyed a sneak peek at his untimely rendezvous.

The party at Renny's was in full swing with music, dancing and everyone in high spirits. Robin and Ruthann waltzed blissfully around the dancefloor stopping to chat with all the guests that wanted to congratulate them. Katrina was sitting in a dark corner of the room smooching Ralph, while Uncle John looked the happiest he'd been in years, dancing with Eileen from the Mace in his arms. However, poor Mosey along with Robin's brother the best man, were doing all they could to try and avoid Lizzie and

Trish, who made it very clear they'd set their sights exclusively on them. It was a great day, even the weather for that time of year couldn't have been better. Heather and Joey were just content to sit back and watch everyone enjoying themselves.

"It's good to see Esther dancing with Stephen," muttered a slightly intoxicated Joey, but Heather didn't reply because it was obvious to her that Esther wasn't interested in him, and nothing she could say or do was going to change that. As soon as the song was over, sure enough, they parted. Stephen went to the bar while Esther waited for the next song to come on, which was one of her favourites, Englebert Humperdinck singing "The Last Waltz", then she inconspicuously made her way out of the party and into the empty front lounge that had only one person standing at the bar sipping brandy out of one of Rita's best glasses and staring right at her. Her heart raced and her body weakened for him.

He walked towards her like a lion about to catch its prey and gently enfolded her in his arms, whispering in her ear, "Will you dance with me, Esther?"

"I'd love to dance with you, Rueben," she replied.

They danced together for a few moments until he took her by the hand and led her out of the lounge and up the stairs. As he took the key out of his pocket, she noticed the little red ceramic heart hanging on the door with the number three engraved on it. Unprepared for him lifting her in his arms, she laughed nervously as he carried her into his room kicking the door shut, as the ceramic heart fell to the floor and broke.

Downstairs in the lounge, Stephen stood all on his own with two glasses of champagne in his hands. He had seen all he needed to and was grief-stricken. When Esther left, he thought she just wanted some time out to be alone and that it would be nice to bring her in a drink. He couldn't believe what he'd witnessed, and it confirmed his worst fear!

"How could she?" he shouted. "And with him of all people!" He shook his head from side to side in shock then knocked back a glass of champagne as if it could ease his pain. "How could she?" he mumbled pacing up and down until eventually he gave in to the fact there was nothing he could do, so he made his way back into the party where everyone had gathered around the dance floor to watch Katrina entertain them all with her Irish dancing; everyone but Esther that was, no one had noticed her missing except Stephen.

The celebrations slowed down, and Tommy bellowed over to Joey to follow him out to the front door. Joey obeyed, knowing Tommy was up to something he didn't want Rita to see. He unlocked the front door and looked up and down a very quiet Dungiven.

"Here Joey, have one of these," he said, handing him a big cigar. "That came all the way from Cuba, one of the finest cigars you'll ever taste."

They lit their cigars and stood looking up at the dark, star-speckled sky, enjoying their quiet time away from all the noise.

"That was a great day, Joey. We're going to miss your Ruthann working here at the weekends. She's a great girl and she's got herself a good husband too. It'll be your Esther next, Joey, in fact, I'm surprised she hasn't been snapped up already for she's a looker."

Joey took a draw of his big cigar blowing the smoke out into the night air which gave him time to think about what Tommy just said. "Well now, Tommy, Esther's the kind of girl that will take her time. She's in no hurry. I think she's more of a career girl myself, you know what I mean? She'll do well for herself, just you wait and see."

But Tommy wanted a bit more information than that. "So, you don't think it'll be happening anytime soon with herself and Stephen then?"

"No, not at the minute, and I'm very glad, for this wedding has cost me a bloody fortune!"

They both laughed until Rita came out to find Tommy having a good time. She gave him a good scolding for leaving her with all the glasses and they all trooped back in, Tommy to wash glasses and Joey to enjoy himself.

Joey found Stephen sitting beside Heather with a very long face. He nudged Heather and asked her if they were at a funeral, pointing at Stephen, but Heather told him to be quiet as they were listening to Ruthann singing her acapella rendition of "Danny Boy." Joey moved closer and could see the tears running down her face, but they were tears of delight. He put his arm around her, and she rested her head on his shoulder. As Ruthann sang the last chorus, Esther discreetly tiptoed back into the party, hoping that no one noticed. No one did except Stephen because he had been waiting. Ruthann ended her amazing performance, and everyone stood to their feet and clapped.

"She has a great voice, Heather," catching sight of his other daughter walking across the dance floor towards Ruthann and kissing her on the cheek. "Look Heather, there's Esther. She looks different?"

Heather looked to see while wiping the tears from her eyes. "Awk, Joey, she's just let her hair down."

But Joey wasn't convinced. "No Heather! She looks… different?"

Stephen overheard and got up from the table.

"Where are you going, Stephen?" asked Joey.

"I'm going home!" And with that, he stormed out.

Both Joey and Heather looked disappointed but again Joey looked over to Esther who was laughing with Katrina and Ralph. "I don't know what you think, Heather but I think Stephen has been blown out!"

Heather just nodded her head.

Esther managed to get a quiet moment with Katrina while Ralph went to the bar, and she told her everything. Katrina was flabbergasted. "But you don't even know him, Esther!"

"I do know him. I love him, and he loves me."

Katrina knew this was something she couldn't advise her on, because when Esther made her mind up about something, that was it. She knew that she had fallen hook, line and sinker for this man and felt sad about it, but the only thing she could do now was to be there for her when it all collapsed.

"I just need you to be happy for me, Kat. Please. You know I've never been with anyone before, not even Stephen. I'm not a slut. I really love him. I have to do this."

Katrina wrapped her arm around her and kissed her on the cheek. "Of course, I know you're not a slut. I do care for you, Esther. I just don't want you getting hurt. I'll be happy for you if this is what you really want."

"Oh, I do! Thank you, Katrina," she said as they hugged one another.

Life had changed for Esther. There was no going back, she was fully committed to Rueben. He was so much more than she had ever dreamed of if that was possible. This was love and now she felt complete!

Six

Rueben and Esther began seeing each other secretly at every opportunity. They met up at the Castle where Rueben spent a lot of his time with military and other governing officials. Esther had never been so happy. Her career was blossoming too, as she had signed a contract to do modelling work in London. Her boss had asked her to model some of the shop's new garments at a Belfast fashion show, not knowing that a director of a London agency was in the audience, and he was immediately drawn to her beauty and stature. She was overwhelmed by it all and couldn't believe the amount of money she'd been offered. It was all very exciting, but when it came to her relationship with Rueben, only Ruthann and Katrina knew what was really going on and she wanted to keep it that way.

Two months passed and the family noticed how jubilant Esther was, putting it all down to her impressive career breakthrough. Even Mosey noticed but quietly found her peculiar behaviour unbearable. Esther hurried home every night from work, had very little to eat then headed right back out again. This had become a frequent occurrence, but tonight, Heather stopped her in her tracks.

"Good evening, Esther!" she said in her motherly authority voice. "Your dinner is in the oven!" but Esther ran on.

Joey glanced at Heather in an uneasy way. "She must be seeing somebody, Heather. I wonder who it is, why won't she tell us?"

Unknown to Joey, Heather had Uncle John's ex-wife, Brenda ringing her to inform her of the gossip that had circled around Dungiven, regarding Esther. Heather wisely chose not to tell Joey anything until she spoke to Esther first, and now seemed to be the right time.

"I think I'll just go up and see if she's alright."

Heather got up from the dinner table and followed her up to her room.

Mosey butted in with only one thing on his mind, "I'll have her dinner if she doesn't want it!"

Heather tapped on Esther's door receiving a loud, "Come in, Mum."

As she opened the door, Esther was sitting at her dressing table brushing her hair. She looked at her mum and sensed this was more than a quick hello. "What's wrong, Mum?"

Heather looked longingly at her, and for a moment saw the little girl she had brought into the world. The little girl with so many hopes and dreams turned into a teenager who wasn't afraid to give her well-thought-out opinions with so much confidence. Now, there she was, this beautiful woman with such a wonderful future ahead of her. Surely everything Brenda told her was lies. Why would Esther ever jeopardise her good reputation for an ageing Yankee who was probably married with children?

"I need to talk to you, Esther and I'm not going to beat around the bush. Brenda phoned me today and told me that people are gossiping about you seeing one of the Yankee officials based at Benbradagh and that you meet with him at the Castle. I'm also told he's quite a bit older than you. Now, please tell me it's not true and it is only gossip, and I'll go back downstairs and finish my dinner."

Esther slowly set her hairbrush down on the dressing table looking very worried at her mother in the mirror. She knew she couldn't lie. "Yes, it is true. I'm so sorry you had to find out this way. I didn't want to hurt anyone, especially you and dad."

Heather closed her eyes and took a deep breath to quietly but anxiously convey her thoughts. "Are you out of your mind? How long has this been going on?"

Esther sat quietly thinking how she could make her mother understand just how much she loved Rueben. Surely of all people and everything that she had been through with her own family, she would understand. She drew breath and began, "I met him a few months ago. It was the day Katrina met Ralph. He was sitting in the back of the jeep, and something happened, Mum, I can't explain it. I've heard people talking about love at first sight. I never thought it would ever happen to me, but it did. I know you don't believe me, but it happened to Rueben too. We love each other so much, and even though it seems so wrong to everyone else, it's not wrong to us."

Heather raised her hand to her brow and shook her head unconvinced of anything Esther had just said. "I can't believe that you've fallen for this… predator, that's what he is a predator. How could you be so stupid?" She raised her voice causing Esther to panic.

"Oh, please keep your voice down, I don't want Dad to know yet, please!"

"So, you think I'm going to keep something like this from your father, do you? Are you kidding me? This man could have a wife and family in the States for all you know."

"I do know, and he hasn't. Is that what you think of me? Do you think I'm that stupid?" Esther hid her face with her hands. She'd had disagreements with her mother before but certainly not like this.

"Right now, Esther, I don't know what to think. I know you have everything to live for and you could have any man you wanted. You've got a modelling contract in London and enough savings to open your own boutique, that was always your dream. You have Stephen who REALLY loves you! Girls would give anything to be in your shoes!" Heather flopped down on the bed bewildered not knowing what to say next. This was the worst-case scenario, but she knew there was more to it, and there was only one way to find out and that was just to ask the question.

"When will everyone get it into their heads I don't love Stephen. I never have! I love Rueben!"

After a moment of silence, Heather asked the dreaded question, "Are you sleeping with him, Esther?" Again silence. "You are, aren't you?"

Esther sat down on the bed beside her and grabbed her hand trying to ease the next blow. "Yes, Mum, I am, I love him. I need him so much it hurts. Surely you understand?"

Heather pushed her hand away with force and glared at her as if she had bathed in cow manure, and that's just how she felt, dirty. Then stood up towering over her, her face red with anger. "Understand? How could you say that? I never slept with your father until I was married, so NO, Esther, I don't understand! I hope you're on the pill young lady because when he dumps you, you won't want to be left with a child on your own! It's tough enough with two parents!"

Esther, now with tears running down her face answered quietly, "You've no need to worry, I am on the pill, and he wouldn't leave me, I know him you don't."

"How could you, Esther? How could you do this to me and your father?"

Heather marched out of the bedroom leaving Esther in floods of tears. How could her own mother make her feel so ashamed when being with Rueben was so precious and beautiful? This was just too much to bear. She couldn't stay there tonight. She regained her strength, packed an overnight bag, quietly sneaked downstairs, through the front door and caught a lift into Dungiven with Uncle John. She felt awkward walking into the Castle now, aware of the snide remarks from staff who obviously discovered their red-hot love affair. She knocked on the door of Rueben's private room, the door opened and there he was with a great big smile on his face, but it didn't take long for him to recognise there was something wrong.

"What's happened, Esther?"

He put his arm around her and took the overnight bag out of her hand leading her into his large, elaborate room. She sat down on the sofa and told him everything that happened, sobbing.

"Oh darling, I'm so sorry. It's because I'm an old Yankee and they want you to be with a young Irish man, or should I say British? They don't know how much I love you. Would you like me to talk with them?"

"No!" she cried. "That would only make things worse. I'm going to stay with you tonight and hopefully, it will all die down by the time I get home from work tomorrow."

Rueben went to pour her a drink and the phone rang. He answered it. "What? Why can't they bring the damn squad in?" He listened attentively.

"What about Sub V9?" … "Okay. Get me on a flight tomorrow!" He set the phone down while Esther tried to digest what had just been said.

"Did you just say you're getting a flight tomorrow? You can't leave me now, I need you."

"And I need you, darling, but I have to go now, listen to me," he held her by the shoulders and looked right into her eyes. "I'll be flying to Washington and then somewhere else, I'm not sure right now."

Esther stopped him, panic-stricken at the thought. "You're going home?"

"Washington is not my home. I told you I have an apartment in New York. Home is here, it's wherever you are my darling. Now please listen to me." He gave her a gentle nudge on the shoulders. "I'll be back in a couple of weeks, and we will have the rest of our lives together. I want you to go on to London, they will love you there, and when you get back, we'll get your dream "Queenies" opened. I should be back by then, but if I'm not, I have an envelope with some money in it for you to help get this up and running fast." He went over to the drawer leaving Esther shell-shocked and took the envelope out and gave it to her. "When I get back, we will never be parted again, that's if you still want this old man?"

"Oh, Rueben, you're only thirty-nine. You're still much younger than the parents! I don't know how I'm going to do all this without you."

He dried her tears with his hand, and she tried to smile, leading him to a kiss and then a passionate kiss. "I love you Esther O'Donnell and don't you ever forget that!"

The next morning, they said their goodbyes with love and tears. Esther tried very hard to keep herself strong and not fall apart even, though she was inside. She left for work wondering how she was going to make it through the day but believing that very soon they would be together, and no one would ever have the power to stop that; it kept her focused. Rueben picked up his passport and suitcase as the door knocked, thinking it was his driver to take him to the airport, but when he opened the door, Heather stood right in front of him looking very cross. He was shocked but really not surprised. He could feel the hate vibe oozing from her, but he pleasantly greeted her the best he could.

"So, you know who I am and why I'm here?" she replied.

"Esther has gone to work, and I have to leave in a few minutes but you're welcome to come in."

Heather spied the suitcase as she walked in looking right around the lavish room. "So, this is where you have your fun with my daughter then. Very upmarket. I wish I could say the same for you. I see by the suitcase it's time for you to go now. Had enough already? Ready for something different or even younger? Or maybe it's time for you to go back to your wife and children, is that it?"

It was plain to see Heather's rage and Rueben knew at that moment nothing he could say or do was going to change her mind. But he was just as angry at her very antagonistic remarks and decided that he wasn't going to take anymore. He was a Commander after all and would never tolerate this kind of behaviour from anyone.

"If you mean what I think you mean, Mrs O'Donnell, I'd then like to remind you that this is a mutual agreement between two consenting adults that are not only, YES passionately involved, but are deeply committed for the rest of our lives. How long that will be no one knows. Yes, I am older! Yes, I am American! And no, I'm not married to anyone only my work that takes up a lot of my time, but Esther and I have discussed that! Does that help at all or are you going to stick with your deluded conclusion that your daughter is better off getting married to someone she doesn't love, living a very unhappy life so she can please you and everyone else who seems to think they have a right to tell her how it should be! OR marry someone she chooses, who adores her and sees that she's not only the most beautiful woman he's ever met but also worth more than every damn vessel out on the Atlantic Sea right now! You'll forgive me if I can't sit down and have tea and a chat but duty calls and there's a war on! I need to be somewhere where my feelings and opinions are respected! But feel free to stay as long as you like." And with that, he stormed out leaving Heather astounded. She certainly hadn't expected that!

Seven

It took a while for the dust to settle, but it did. Heather hadn't told Joey about Esther's affair as she believed it would all end soon, but she did tell Esther about the 'fireworks display' that took place at the castle between herself and Rueben. No matter what was happening, Esther had no choice but to concentrate on her career now. Modelling contracts poured in after her London debut, she even had to turn down some, unable to keep up with the demand. Newspapers wanted interviews because not only had she become an overnight celebrity, but she also had the good fortune to purchase the boutique she previously worked in, and named it "Queenies", the title she gave it all those years ago when she conceived it in her mind as a child. It was all very overwhelming and wonderful, but where was Rueben? She needed him. Weeks turned into months. Eventually, she received flowers on her birthday with a note saying, 'I love you and miss you. I'll be back soon. RR.' That was just enough to re-ignite her strength to keep going.

Stephen had been a great help to her in setting up the shop, and for a while, he hoped that there might still be a chance for the two of them to get together now that Rueben was out of sight, but Ruthann and Katrina knew only too well how much she was missing him, and that out of sight didn't necessarily mean out of mind. But no one spoke about Rueben, hoping that Esther's infatuation would all pass away inconspicuously. It was like a dirty little secret that nobody wanted to talk about. Unable to release her true feelings, the pain that built up in her was like a tumour that grew, the more she suppressed her pain, but she had to because no one wanted to know. It was cruel. Why was everyone so cruel? She began to see people in a different light.

It was a quiet day at Queenies and it gave Esther the chance to organise some of the new garments that had just come in. Stephen came rushing in with a big smile on his face. "Did I leave my screwdriver here, Esther?"

"Yes, it's under the counter. I found it lying at the back door." He went behind the counter to grab it. "Why are you all smiles?" she asked curiously.

"Oh, it's just a good day, that's all." His reply made her all the more curious but he distracted her thoughts as he went on to say, "Hey girl! You're famous now. Eileen has been showing your photos in the magazines to everyone that comes into the shop."

"Oh, bless her heart," she said earnestly. "Listen, Stephen, I just want to thank you for everything you did for me here getting Queenies up and running. I don't think I could have done it without you."

Stephen, not having seen the humble side of Esther in a long time, if ever, deliberated and then asked cautiously, "I couldn't help but notice you haven't been yourself since you got back from London. Are you alright?"

She could see by his eyes that he cared but maybe not the way he used too. "It's hard to keep anything from you. I just wish I could have fallen in love with you, it would have been so much easier!" Her eyes filled with tears yearning to talk about Rueben but knowing his name was a no-go area.

"I think you'll be happy to know I've given up on that idea now," he replied. She looked surprised. "Never sell yourself short, Esther. You're too good!" Then he opened the door and left, but she called him back.

"Do you fancy going to the Renny's tonight? I'd love some company and a chat."

"I'm sorry, Esther I've made other arrangements."

And with that, he quickly exited the boutique leaving her astonished. Ruthann passed him on her way in, but Esther didn't even notice her, busy wondering why Stephen was acting so oddly; he had always made time for her.

"Esther, I have some great news for you!"

Esther jumped, lifting her head sharply and without thinking she responded, "What! Is it Rueben? Have you seen him?"

Ruthann looked at her just as startled. This had nothing to do with Rueben and her question, along with her pale complexion, was concerning.

"I'm afraid not, Esther. It has nothing at all to do with Rueben. Are you alright? You look so sad."

Esther couldn't keep her feelings in any longer. "Oh, Ruthann, I'm sorry, it's just that I miss him so much. Where is he? I haven't heard a word since he sent me the flowers and card on my birthday. He could be dead for all I know."

She walked over to the shop door, locked up and then sat down on the floor with her head in her hands. Ruthann was tired of seeing her sister like this and angry that Rueben hadn't got in touch with her. If only he knew how heartless and cruel this was on her, and how it was taking its toll on her physically, with her weight loss and sad face.

"If he was dead you would know about it, Esther. It would be all over the news. What does Ralph say? Surely, he knows where he is?"

"He hasn't heard a thing," she replied taking a tissue out of her pocket and wiping her eyes.

A worried Ruthann sat down beside her on the floor and took her by the hand. "Remember what I told you that day in the bedroom after you'd just met him?"

Esther nodded, knowing she was right about the tears, but it still didn't make any difference, she loved him even more now.

"I told you there'd be lots of tears and lots of tears there's been. Get yourself out of this while you still can, Esther. This moping isn't good for you. Mum's worried about you too, she knows your heart's broken, but she doesn't want to say anything in case there's a row and Dad finds out. She's trying very hard to keep this from him because he'll go crazy!"

Esther looked at her confused. "But he's been fixing more of their jeeps, so he can't despise them that much?"

"It's only because they're paying him well, Esther."

"I can't get out of this, Ruthann! He has my heart and that's a big piece missing from me. I do wish he'd give it back so that I can get on with my life!" she cried putting her head down again.

Ruthann hugged her and proceeded to tell her the good news. "He'd better give it back because very soon you're going to be Aunty Esther!"

Esther jumped to her feet. "What!" She took Ruthann by the hand and pulled her up. "That's great news. I'm so happy for you, and Robin!"

Esther shut up shop and the pair of them went to Renny's to get a bite to eat and tell Rita the good news, and for a few hours, her mind had a break from Rueben Redpath. After the celebrations, Esther went home but felt worn out. The fast life she had been accustomed to in the past few months was starting to take its toll.

Heather sat at the kitchen table doing her usual weekly admin for Joey. She watched Esther saunter slowly and miserably through the back door, concerned at her sad appearance. She knew the source of it was down to Rueben, but still refused to have that conversation, fearful it could make matters worse. Esther walked over to the big chair beside the small front window dragging her feet the whole way and threw herself down as if she had collapsed.

"Did you and Ruthann have a nice time?" Heather waited for a response but just got a grunt. She tried again, "Isn't it great news about the baby?"

Esther managed to say yes, making it obvious she didn't want to partake in any conversation, only wanting to rest but just before she got to close her eyes, she spied a strange girl over at Uncle John's. Her curiosity got the better of her and she leapt up to have a better look. "Who's that girl over at Uncle John's?" she asked, peering out of the window.

"Are you only noticing her now? Why that's John's new housekeeper, Sandy George. She's a lovely girl. One of the Georges from the Gate Lodge, you know them?"

Esther looked puzzled. "No, I don't know them."

"She and Stephen have been seeing each other. Didn't you know?"

Esther had no idea about this and instantly felt betrayed that he hadn't told her earlier. So that's why he was so reserved and happy. It was only now she grasped how much she was missing out on, with her thoughts continually absorbed by a man who didn't even have the decency to make any form of contact with her. Many days and nights she'd waited on him like a lovelorn puppy, yet every time she got angry, she remembered all the loving things he had told her. But did she trust him? She did, and once again deep down inside she knew that wherever he was, whatever he was doing, he was missing her too, she could feel it. It was like they had a supernatural bond that couldn't be broken.

"Your dad is over the moon about becoming a granda."

Again, Esther didn't respond. She felt so drowsy.

"I am worried about you, Esther; you're getting far too thin. I hope you're not dieting for those photographs. I know you've had a lot on your plate, love, what with Queenies and…"

Heather kept on talking until suddenly, Esther jumped up from the chair. A small white van had driven up and parked on their driveway. Two suspicious-looking men with woollen caps jumped out and quickly made their way up the drive to Joey and Mosey at the garage. They were definitely not there to talk about cars. Alarm bells went off in Esther's head.

"Mum! Quick! There's something not right!"

"What do you mean?" Heather replied anxiously getting up from the table and running over to the window to

Esther, and then following her to the back window. They watched as the men argued with Joey. "I don't like the look of this, Esther. Where's our Mosey? I'm phoning the police," she said, running to the phone.

"No, wait Mum! You can't! Not yet just wait a minute!"

The men left as quickly as they had arrived. Joey took a minute and then made his way into the house while Mosey ran over to get Uncle John and Stephen. A very shaken Joey sat down at the table unable to speak.

"What happened, Joey? Who were those men?" Heather shouted, feeling close to hysteria.

Joey took a minute to get his breath to answer, "I've been threatened! By the Provo's. They told me they'd shoot me if I ever fixed one of them jeeps again. They told me I was a traitor for marrying a Prod and bringing my children up Prods. I thought they were going to shoot me there and then, that's the truth, Heather."

The door banged open and Uncle John, Mosey and Stephen ran in. "Where are the bastards?" yelled Uncle John. "I'll shoot them!" he said, brandishing his double-barrelled shotgun.

"They're gone, John. There'll be no shooting, and no police involved, do yous hear me? Them boys mean business. They called me a British-loving bastard doing the work for the British government. From now on, there'll be none of them damn jeeps anywhere near this house, that's the end of it. I knew them bloody Yankees would cause me trouble. I don't want anyone saying a word of this to anyone, do yous all hear me?"

"It's my fault, Dad," cried a very scared Mosey.

"It's not your fault son, don't even think that way. It's my fault. They were paying well, and I got greedy. Just shows you, money isn't everything!"

Everyone looked horrified. Esther began to feel an overwhelming surge of guilt coming over her as if it was all her fault, wanting to confess everything but not wanting to hurt anyone or make the situation worse. It was all becoming a nightmare, and this disturbing situation was forcing her to make major life-changing decisions.

They all calmed down as much as they could and Mosey headed up to his room. Esther quietly made her way into the front room leaving Joey, Heather and John to chat about whether they should leave their home or not, but Joey was strongly against that; proper security measures around the house made more sense to him, as this was their home and not even the Provos were going to change that.

Stephen followed Esther into the front room, and as she sat down on the couch, he lingered in the doorway. "I can't imagine what you're going through, Esther," he said sympathetically.

But Esther snapped back at him, "You're right. You can't!"

The unwelcome vibes just made Stephen want to leave. "I'm going to head back over to the house, but I just wanted to say-" he paused. "Well, I don't know what I wanted to say."

Esther glared at him as if he was the enemy coming to gloat. "Oh, come on, Stephen! We both know exactly what you wanted to say! You wanted to say I told you so, Esther, you're a fool Esther, now you need me more than ever, Esther! Well maybe you're right, maybe I do need you,

Stephen, but only as a friend. A friend that cares enough to want to know what's happening in your life and is happy to talk without pretending everything's cool, everything's fine! All that rot!" She stood up, feeling exasperated and defeated while all he could do was watch and listen in shock, as she went on, "You know my heart's broken, but today it's even more broken and I didn't think that was possible. So go on, Mr Kind and Dependable McCarthy, the one who can give the nice, sensible kind of love! Well good for you!" and she turned her back on him.

Stephen stood astounded, unprepared for such an outburst at that moment but replied honestly, "Why do you always have to be so hostile towards me? I thought we were getting on well. I'm putting this down to what's just happened Esther, and now I'll go!"

As he went to walk out, Esther hollered, "Yeah, run on to Miss George. You'll never have problems with her!"

He laughed a sarcastic laugh and answered her calmly, "I'm not foolish enough to believe for one second you're jealous, Esther."

"You could have told me, Stephen!" she yelled. "That's what friends do!"

He shook his head in amazement. "I didn't think for one minute you'd be the slightest bit interested."

"Oh, shut the door on the way out!" she shouted, closing her eyes and taking a deep breath, as Stephen left, banging the door.

Eight

It was the Sunday after that awful day Joey had been threatened. The O'Donnell household was filled with fear and dread, especially Heather. She had begun to think that every car passing the cottage was assigned by the Provos to spy on them, but she tried to keep to her usual routine. Joey sat at the top of the table as usual and read the paper, or at least that's what he wanted her to think, while Esther just sat staring out of the window and that was now a common practice.

Joey pulled his paper down and looked at Heather for a few seconds before asking, "Are you not going to church this morning?"

"Of course, I'm not Joey. I'm not going anywhere." She didn't want to leave the house and had become so uptight, checking to see where everyone was at all times. It was like an obsession, like it was her job to patrol and protect her family, becoming smothering rather than mothering. "What's happening with the world right now?" she asked, as if pleading for the solution. "I thought living here at the bottom of a mountain in the heart of the countryside in Northern Ireland would be one of the safest places to live! Instead, we have an American naval base on our very doorstep talking to ships on the Atlantic Sea about Russia, with whispers of having nuclear weapons, and now we're being threatened by the IRA because you married me and tried to earn an honest living, so they want to shoot you? It's like we're living in the times of Armageddon. Nothing makes sense anymore. I feel like a prisoner, Joey, and I can't live like this anymore! We need to leave!"

Joey could see how stressed she'd become, and he needed to calm her down. "We're not going anywhere, Mrs O," he said kindly and lovingly. "This will all die down soon enough, love. Them Yankees won't be there forever, and as for the IRA, we'll keep our heads down and keep ourselves to ourselves. It won't always be like this; you wait and see." He kissed her. "Getting stressed is only going to make things worse." He looked out through the window and up at the mountain. "And as for nuclear weapons? I doubt that very much. Soon things will be back to the way they used to be, you mark my word love," trying hard to reassure her. He then sat down at the table again, pretending to look at the newspaper. "You should've gone to church love."

Joey was worried too but tried to hide it for everyone's sake and only Esther could see it. She understood her mother's concerns and it was tough for them all living with the fear that this could happen again, or even worse. The circumstances had forced her to get her priorities in order, so she declined an offer of a modelling contract again in London because she didn't want to leave the family at this time, and also she needed to be at home in case Rueben returned. Even though her hopes of that happening were starting to fade and even if he did, she knew their relationship would have to end. It would break her heart but at least he would still be around, she hoped.

She couldn't put up with the tense atmosphere in the house any longer and felt she needed to break free for a breather. "I need to think!" she stated, and after all these years, the family knew exactly what that meant, the cowgate. "I'm just going out for a walk up to the cowgate, Mum, so don't be worrying. I'll be back."

It was a cold and gloomy November day, so she wrapped up warm in her sheepskin coat, a scarf and hat, and strolled up to the cowgate, jumping up on it just like she always did, to admire the same spectacular view that she never tired off. Remembering Katrina that beautiful day now over two years ago, lying on the ground looking up at Ralph, she began to laugh. The thought naturally retrieved the memory of meeting the handsome stranger who captured her heart the very instant their eyes met. There and then she decided that from that moment on, she had to move on with her life; it wasn't so much choice but necessity as it wasn't just herself, she had to think about, but the whole family. It was her turn to be the strong one now that she had seen how fragile her parents were at this time.

Everything was so peaceful, just peace, perfect peace until something very strange happened. She could see a Land Rover in the distance racing up the road. At first, she thought it was Uncle John's vehicle but then she realised it was a different shape. She began to panic and jumped down from the gate, praying it wasn't the IRA for her dad. She stood rigid not knowing what to do, but thankfully it raced on past the cottage and she breathed a sigh of relief. As it got closer to her, the driver made an emergency stop, and her heart raced with fear until he pulled the navy baseball cap off his head, and she realised it was Rueben. He jumped out of the Land Rover and without saying a word, lifted her up in his arms, and in response she put her arms around his neck as if it was the most natural thing in the world to do. He opened the passenger side door and set her in. The power in her body left, and with a combination of joy and shock, there was absolutely nothing she could do or wanted to do; she was his.

There was no communication between them as he drove rampantly up the mountain, apart from his hand holding hers so tightly as if to say everything was going to be alright. Before she knew it, they were at the top of Benbradagh. He drove on past the base to a remote spot where you could see nothing but the rugged terrain for miles. There in front of them was a tent with a table and chair beside it. He got out and quickly paraded around, opening her door and lifting her into his arms.

She finally managed to speak, "Where did you come from and what are you doing?" barely able to take in what was happening.

He stopped and looked into her eyes, "I'm back and I'm never leaving you again!"

His words released her tears, and she became so overcome with emotion that all the hurt and anger she had shut away turned to vulnerability, and she knew she couldn't protest his desire for her. He lay her down on a blanket in the tent, kissing her so passionately that never had she felt so willingly helpless, surrendering herself to be seduced in such a way that even the North wind beating off the mountain had no comparison to his valour and desire for her. She yielded helplessly to his every need, her heart pounding recklessly. They were one!

Listening to the sound of the wind while she watched Rueben getting dressed, made her feel that every stress and strain of that year had departed. He looked at her adoringly before leaving the tent, took a packet of cigarettes out of his trouser pocket, lit one up and inhaled loudly. This was new to Esther; she had never seen him smoke before. He gazed over the horizon as it was starting to get dark, but that made their cosy niche feel even cosier.

"I've never seen you smoke before?" But he didn't answer so she tried again, "What are you thinking about? You need to talk to me, Rueben."

He turned and looked at her. "Come over here beautiful lady," he requested politely.

Esther wrapped the blanket tightly around her delicate form and wandered over to him. He snuggled his arm around her and with the other, he pointed out to the panorama. "Look at all this, how beautiful it is. Feel that wind on your face, Esther. It's like an awakening!"

She looked at him puzzled, "An awakening?"

"Yes, an awakening. Like something within you that you thought had died coming alive again! Something so extraordinary, you're not even sure how to withstand it!" Again, he stared while Esther just looked at him stunned by what he'd just said. This wasn't the Rueben she knew, and she wondered what had happened to make him say something so bizarre.

"Like what Rueben?"

He didn't answer but remained staring out into the big space. Esther began to get irritated by his conduct. She had no idea what was going on but needed answers and fast, not all the muddled-up mumbo jumbo, but then she saw tears in his eyes, and he continued, "It's like an outflow of all the filth and profanity of mankind. It consumes you, every inch of you until you can't take anymore, then it leaves you like it was never there in the first place, but it was!"

This was too much for Esther to grasp. She could only reply by her actions and ran into the tent quickly to get dressed, shouting, "You're scaring me. I don't understand all this!"

He seemed unmoved and shouted back to her, "Of course, you don't understand, but don't be scared, darling. If I could stay here for the rest of my life with you then I would die happy knowing my life had been fulfilled." He turned toward the tent. "Anyway, how could someone as beautiful and innocent as you understand how brutal life can be?"

That was it! Esther had enough. How dare he say that after everything she had been through? It was time he heard what she had to say, and she screamed to him at the top of her voice, "OH REALLY! Do you honestly think I have no idea how brutal life can be? Really! You've been gone for over a year with no contact so how the hell would you know?" She managed to get dressed and stormed out of the tent straight over to him and slapped him on the face. He was shocked by her rage, but she hadn't finished. "I waited and waited on you. I even turned down work because of you, just in case you would come back. I was so worried I thought you might be dead. I'm beginning to think Mum was right, you are married and I'm a fool! How could you?" She hysterically beat him on the chest, but he grabbed her hands as her anger turned to sorrow. "Why did you leave me when I needed you so much? You never even rang me!"

The tears fell from his eyes also as he watched her pain, and he felt helpless. There was so much he needed to tell her, but this wasn't the time or the place. "I can only say how sorry I am, Esther. I needed you so much too. At this minute I can only tell you some of it was work, but some of it was personal too. At the right time, I'll tell you everything, I promise, trust me. Please don't be angry with me, not now! I told you the last time we were together that we would never be parted again, and I meant it."

She stopped him quickly, "I could never put myself through this pain again, Rueben."

He strolled over to the table, sat down, lit up another cigarette and began to fight back, "It hasn't been all bad for you! You've been in magazines and newspapers and now you've got Queenies. Do you know how hard it was for me knowing how your life was progressing, and I couldn't be there with you? I couldn't be there at the opening of the shop or escort you to London. It broke my heart, and I couldn't do anything about it! It was hell!"

Everything went quiet and the roles reversed. Esther stood staring out over the landscape while Rueben smoked his cigarette. She knew by his tone he meant every word. "I had no idea you felt that way," she cried as she went over to him and sat down at his feet. "You've changed, Rueben. Something big has happened to you. What is it?"

He couldn't tell her. All he could do was hold her as they wept together. "I love you so much, Esther O'Donnell."

"I love you too, Rueben Redpath."

He let go of her and sprinted over to the Land Rover, took something out from the driver's side and sprinted back, getting down on one knee and asking,
"Will you marry this old Yankee, Esther?"

He opened the little box and there was the most beautiful diamond ring she had ever seen. He put it on her engagement finger. Esther cried even more.

"I can't Rueben, I'm sorry, I can't even see you again after this, never mind marry you."

He looked horrified by her answer. "What are you talking about?"

She told him all about the threat on her father's life, how none of the jeeps could ever go near their house again, and how they could never be seen together as Joey's life was at stake. Rueben was infuriated as well as confused, he didn't know anything about this. "I know everything so why was I not informed about this?" he demanded in his military voice.

Esther replied with sarcasm in her voice, "Because nobody knows, Commander Redpath Sir! That's why!"

He gave her a quick grin knowing she was the only person who could get away with speaking to him like that. They discussed it over and over again. "I can't believe there's nothing we can do. I have money, power!" he shouted with frustration. But Esther's reply finished it,

"Not enough to stop the war in Northern Ireland, Rueben!"

He eventually calmed down, but heartbroken insisted she kept the ring as a reminder of how much he would always love her. She agreed, but she also had a request, "I can only keep going knowing that you're staying at Benbradagh."

He agreed reluctantly, knowing how hard that was going to be, seeing her but being unable to hold her or talk to her was a lot to ask.

"I need to go now. Mum will be frantic."

"I'll never stop loving you, Esther."

"This stupid country is so cruel!" she replied.

Nine

The weeks went by, but it certainly hadn't eased Esther's burdens. Everyone tried to go on as normally as possible, but the escalating troubles in Northern Ireland were only making things more difficult. Esther tried to keep herself busy working all hours, only content knowing that Rueben was still around, and she could get secret glimpses of him from time to time. He purposely drove by her shop many times in his Land Rover, wearing his navy baseball cap so that no one could recognise him, only Esther.

It had been another busy day at the boutique as people would come from far and wide just to get a glimpse of the famous Esther O'Donnell. There were still a few customers trying on some clothes in the changing rooms when Stephen came darting into the shop with some very exciting news. "Your mum sent me, Esther. It's great news. You're an Aunty!" Esther jumped up and down with joy. "Ruthann had a baby boy this morning and both are doing great!"

This was just what the family needed, and for a little while, it seemed that everything had returned to normal. Heather and Joey were so happy about being grandparents that the threat to Joey's life took a back seat. Stephen seemed to be happy with Sandy and that kept him occupied, and there was talk that Uncle John was dating Eileen which was definitely a turn-up for the books. It wasn't long before the day of the Christening came around and sure enough, Uncle John was there, arm in arm with Eileen, as proud as punch making a statement that they were now a very happy couple. Esther and Mosey were Godparents on Ruthann's side of the family, as was

Robin's brother and cousin on their side. Lots of photos were taken outside the church and everyone wanted to see Master Thomas Joseph Harvey in his long white Christening gown.

As Esther came out of the church, she felt someone watching her. She looked across the road and saw Rueben sitting in a clapped-out car staring right at her. Once again, their eyes locked together, neither of them able to concentrate on anything else, smiling flirtatiously at each other, unaware that Heather was watching.

Once again, the Christening celebrations were held at Renny's. Joey stood proudly at the bar holding his new grandson showing him off to Rita.

"Isn't he handsome, Rita? Thomas Joseph. They named him Joseph after me you know, Joseph." Rita tittered as she had never seen Joey so proud before. "Now watch him when I sing."

Rita was duty-bound to his request and watched Thomas smile as Joey sang, "You are my sunshine my only sunshine," until Ruthann saved the day, and she managed to reclaim Thomas from his doting grandad, laughing as she explained that he was smiling because he was releasing wind, not Granda's singing, but Joey wasn't convinced.

Tommy made his way over to Joey with two glasses of whiskey. "This will wet the baby's head, Joey. Cheers." And they knocked it back. Tommy wiped his mouth and turning solemnly to Joey, asked, "Tell me this, have you heard who's bought the Castle?"

Joey looked shocked; he didn't know the Castle was for sale. "It couldn't be anybody from around here because they couldn't afford it," he said laughing. They went on to chat about the troubles, Joey being very careful not to say a word of what had happened to him. "We'll get another wee refill when the wife's not looking!" Tommy whispered, winking his eye and nodding his head hastily then making his way behind the bar, in response to Rita's high-pitched demand.

The celebrations continued into early evening and then everyone started to leave, including the Harvey family as it was time to get Thomas into his own cot for his night's sleep. The rest of the O'Donnells finished off their drinks.

"It was very good of Tommy to let us use the back room today," said Heather, happy to see her family so relaxed. "But it is Sunday, and we would need to go."

Just then Tommy came over to them with an ice-bucket holding a bottle of champagne in it, and four champagne glasses. He set it down on their table. They all look confused.

"We didn't order that, Tommy," said Joey looking worried.

"I know you didn't, Joey but that gentleman at the bar did."

They all looked up and there was Rueben, as bold as brass sitting at the bar. He smiled down at them and raised his brandy glass. "To wet the baby's head, isn't that what they say? Cheers, Slainte."

Esther felt a cold sweat come over her and wanted to disappear knowing his accent alone was enough to infuriate her father, and she was right.

"Tommy, you can tell that Yankee that we don't need his fancy champagne to celebrate."

Esther closed her eyes and waited for the explosion. This was not the way this lovely day was meant to end. How stupid of Rueben to do that. What was he thinking? She couldn't make out if he was genuinely being kind or wanting her attention. Either way, he of all people should have known better. Tommy was flabbergasted, having no idea what was going on. Rueben was a well-paying guest of theirs and even though he didn't know a lot about him, he knew he was a well-to-do Naval official who preferred his privacy. It worked well for both parties.

"Come on, Joey, we're leaving!" Heather stated forcefully, afraid of Joey losing his temper. They all got up aware that they had to walk past Rueben to get to the exit.

"I'm so sorry," said a deflated Rueben. "I only wanted to congratulate you."

"What's going on?" asked Tommy.

"You don't need to know, Tommy," replied a flustered Joey. "We'll go quietly."

Mosey led the way, then Heather, Joey and Esther. But Joey stopped at Rueben. Esther looked at him with panic on her face. Joey glared at Rueben speaking very quietly to him, "You Yankees may drive past my house but make damn sure yous never stop again. Now I'm not sure what you lot are doing up our mountain, but this I do know, you're not welcome!"

Rueben couldn't believe what he heard but it put everything Esther had told him into perspective. He could only shake his head in bewilderment. Heather pulled Joey by the arm, "Come on, Joey!" while Esther pushed him on.

"Go on, Dad!" Then he went.

Tommy and Rita look on with their mouths open not sure what to do, and not sure what Joey had just said to Rueben, but they knew it wasn't good. Esther stopped by him and whispered softly, so they couldn't hear, "What did you do that for? You've made things worse!"

Rueben could see how angry she was and realised he had made a big mistake. "I'm sorry, I didn't mean to. I had no idea they would react like that."

She went to walk on, but he pulled her back. Rita caught sight of this and hovered around in close proximity wiping the counter. "I have to go away but only for a few days. I'll be back. I love you."

That made her even angrier. "You said that the last time. I can't do this Rueben, please." Her eyes filled with tears. "I love you no matter what. I can't predict what's going to happen now!" She dashed out through the door leaving Rueben baffled by what she'd just said. He wondered what she meant by that but there was nothing he could do.

Rita started clearing away the glasses close by and asked if he was alright, hoping to find out a little more of what was really going on, but Rueben sipped the last of his brandy and went to his room. Tommy made his way over to Rita, asking, "What the hell just happened there, Rita? What's got into Joey?"

Rita had a suspicious look on her face and replied, "I'm not sure what's going on there, Tommy, but I can tell you this, Esther O'Donnell seems very fond, maybe even too fond of him up there," she said, pointing upwards to Rueben's room. "I've seen how they look at each other."

Tommy shook his head and tutted, "Ah, so that's why. It all starting to make sense now!"

Ten

It had been a busy Friday for Esther, and it was coming to the end of the working day. She was counting her earnings at the till, getting ready to close up shop for the evening when the phone rang. She answered and it was Katrina looking to call in to see her before she closed.

"Is everything ok?" she asked her, relieved that the answer was yes. "Alright, I won't lock up until you arrive. Bye."

As she put the phone down, the shop door opened and a very attractive woman in her early forties walked in. Esther greeted her and went on counting. She glanced at the woman and then recognised her, Marianne Stellabrass. She caught Marianne glancing back at her. Esther found this very odd but watched how she took out a few blouses and held them up to her. She settled on a blue chiffon blouse and went over to the mirror, looking undecided.

"Feel free to try it on; that fabric is so delicate. The colour suits you."

But Marianne walked up to the counter with it in her hand. "No, thank you, I'll just buy it."

She took a purse out of a very large, fashionable Mary Quant handbag and handed her a twenty-pound note. Esther put the blouse neatly in a bag but had a strange sensation that Marianne's eyes were piercing through her.

"I didn't have time to go to Belfast today and needed something quick for tonight's celebrations."

Esther got her change together but politely asked, just to make conversation, "How lovely. What's the celebration? Is it your birthday?"

Marianne abruptly answered, "Oh, haven't you heard? I've bought the Castle." Esther was taken back by this disclosure. "Oh, yes, and I'm having the Lord Mayor of Belfast at it, and our local MPs. Oh, and of course, some of the military and naval officials from Benbradagh. That lovely Commander Rueben Redpath is coming too. My, he does like a party, doesn't he? And a little smooch too. Keep the change deary!" And with that, she paced out the door.

Esther stood stiff with anger not knowing whether to cry or die, he couldn't do this to her, but Marianne was his age and very attractive, rich enough to buy a Castle, and most of all very available. Thoughts of the two of them together bombarded her, but thankfully Katrina came in just in time for the show down. "That bitch!"

Katrina looked around, maybe not as stunned as she should be, knowing Esther's crazy conduct all those years. "I do hope you're not talking about me?" and she laughed, but Esther's straight face stayed angry.

"Marianne Stellabrass! She's as much as told me she's going out with Rueben. She's bought the Castle and there's big celebrations there tonight and Rueben will be there."

Katrina listened to her rant about his antics on Sunday past at the Christening, sympathising with her as much as she could although, she now knew how much Rueben wanted to be with Esther and couldn't. Esther had previously confided everything to her, from the threat on her dad's life to the ring and the marriage proposal, so Katrina understood just how much they loved one another but couldn't be together. She also had the benefit of

Ralph's inside information and tonight she had some more news for her.

"I don't believe he's seeing her, Esther; she's just trying to make you jealous. But what I do know is this, he has bought the Castle with her. They're partners. Did Marianne not tell you that?"

Esther wasn't quite sure what to think of that bombshell. Was this a good thing or a bad thing? She still had her queries about the two of them together and that was too much to bear.

"That's it! I've made my mind up, Kat. I'm leaving. I can't take any more. I'm packing my bags and I'm going to accept that offer in London, the one I turned down. I need to get away. I can't watch him with someone else."

And that was it, her mind was made up.

Katrina was happy for her, although she had plans of her own. "I have news for you, Esther. I'm leaving too!"

Esther walked slowly around the counter to her. "What do you mean you're leaving?" scared of her reply.

"Ralph and I are getting married in Arkansas next month and that's where I'm going to live. I don't want to bring children up here in this country; besides I've spoken to Ralph's family on the phone and they're so lovely. They make me feel as if I'm one of them, and in a way I am."

Esther embraced her, knowing how different life was going to be without her best friend. How she would miss her. Katrina put her hand in her bag and pulled out a bottle of wine. "So, celebrations are in order all round then. Never mind Ms Stellabrass."

"If you don't mind, Katrina, I don't feel like it. I just want to go home. I'm so overwhelmed by all this, and I've such a lot to do and so do you. I'm going to miss you so much, but Ralph is a good man, and I know you'll both be very happy together."

Katrina felt a little odd; she had an uneasy feeling about Esther but wasn't sure why, but they did their reminiscing before saying their goodbyes. There were lots of tears, promising each other faithfully to stay in touch.

"Esther, please be careful. Try to make the right choices."

Esther did try to make the right choices, even though she had acted quickly, she felt it was for the best. She closed Queenies and everyone in the town was shocked knowing how successful the business was, but they also knew Esther O'Donnell was born for bigger and better things. She packed her bags and managed to get a flight booked to Heathrow the day after next, leaving Heather to sort out all the stock and liaise with the estate agent. Heather didn't mind, in fact, she was secretly relieved though curious, knowing Rueben had now based himself in Dungiven having bought the Castle.

The evening before Esther was due to leave, Stephen called over to say goodbye and offered to take her for a farewell drink at Renny's.

"Won't Sandy mind?" she remarked mischievously.

"NO!" he replied raising his voice.

She could see he was upset, not because of her remark but because she was leaving. No matter what arguments or disagreements they had, there was still a sense of familiarity and understanding between them. They made their way to

Renny's laughing about some of the funny times they shared together and, on a sadder note, Katrina leaving to get married in America.

When they got to Renny's it seemed quite busy, but Stephen managed to find a seat for them both and he went to the bar while Esther made herself comfortable. She looked around believing Rueben wouldn't be there especially with it so busy, even though a big part of her wanted him to be. It was then she heard a woman's loud laughter and without thinking, she immediately turned and there was Marianne sitting at a table with Rueben. Jealousy raged within her along with sadness.

Stephen set the drinks down and asked, "Are you alright? Do you want to go somewhere else?"

"I just want to go over there and throw these drinks all over them."

Rueben got up and walked directly over to them. "It's good to see you, Esther. I hear you're leaving in the morning?"

She could tell he was nervous trying to say the right thing, but there was nothing he could say that would please her, not when Marianne was there. "I'm sure your pleased I'm leaving. You've left that Marianne Slapperface sitting over there all on her own, that's not very gentlemanly of you, is it?"

He could see she was seething and knew to tread carefully. "Marianne is only a business partner, Esther," he replied cautiously.

"Oh, is she indeed. I think you'd better inform her of that cause she thinks differently. Anyway, you've got a big Castle all to yourselves now, how lovely for you both!" Her voice started to get louder. "Was there ever a time you were going to tell me about your secret business venture or was that just between you and the merry widow over there?"

Everyone in the bar was now starting to look over, and of all times, Lizzy and Trish had front-row seats absorbed in the performance. Rita called to Tommy, and they watched unobtrusively in the background.

"I can't get talking to you about anything, Esther! You don't want to know!" answered Rueben, resorting to his Commander's voice but this was enough to provoke Esther to stand to her feet and look him right in the eye.

"And I thought you were away when all the time you were playing monopoly with her!"

Rueben went to walk away but turned back to her and yelled, "I was away, but you hadn't noticed!"

Stephen felt very uncomfortable and tried hard to get Esther to leave.

"Go away, back to your partner, Rueben. She's more your age anyway. I think you were made for each other."

Everyone was now focused on this love triangle but neither Rueben nor Esther cared. They were both hurting.

"You don't mean that, Esther! Damn it! We were made for each other, and you know it!"

Stephen took Esther by the arm and practically dragged her out while Esther squealed, "I'm tired of all this and I'm leaving!"

The show was over, but the gossip started. Rueben headed back over to Marianne who had enjoyed every minute of them arguing. He apologised to her, and they both felt it was better to leave. Tommy and Rita had all their questions answered while Trish turned to Lizzie, eyes wide open in amazement, over the moon to see such action in Renny's.

"Well, who seen that one coming? Miss Queenie and the Big Yankee. Who'd have thought, eh?" Lizzie shook her head with envious disgust.

Eleven

Esther arrived back at the cottage from the showdown at Renny's. She knew now she had to tell Mum and Dad everything that had happened, sure they would hear it from someone else otherwise. She burst through the back door startling Heather who was washing up dinner dishes.

"Where's Dad?" she cried, tears running down her face as she sat down at the kitchen table. "I need to talk to you both! It's really important."

Heather was becoming concerned at the state she was in. "What on earth has happened, Esther?"

"I've got something important I need to tell you and Dad urgently."

"Surely you're not thinking of staying now, Esther?"

"No, Mum! I can't wait to go and get away from here."

It was plain to see the look of relief on Heather's face, even though she didn't want to show it. "Your dad's on the phone talking to Rita. Why? What's all this about?"

"OH NO! He knows, Mum, about Rueben. Rita's telling him what happened!"

Rita had rung Joey and told him everything she knew, reckoning that he had a right to know. Joey calmly set the phone down but rumbled within like a volcano about to erupt. He heard Esther's voice in the kitchen and raged in like a wild bear.

"What the hell's going on, Esther? I've had Rita on the phone telling me about the pantomime in Renny's! And that Yankee you've been seeing behind my back. You knew as well, Heather, and you didn't think to tell me?"

Heather looked to the floor and nodded her head in shame. "I know Joey, I'm sorry I should have told you, but you have enough on your plate…"

"Stop there, I'm the man of the house, you know I need to know these things so don't give me that bullshit! So that's why he was all pally, sending down champagne and congratulating us, because my daughter's been sleeping with him, and everyone knew but me!"

"It's not like that, Dad!" Esther roared back at him. "I love him. I've loved him from the first time I laid eyes on him."

He answered back sharply, his voice getting louder, "And when was that exactly?"

"A few years ago. The day Katrina met Ralph. It was him that brought the jeep to Mosey that Sunday morning and…"

She didn't get to finish her sentence as he banged his fist on the table and Esther jumped with fright. "WHAT? You're telling me this has been going on all this time. Are you off your head, Esther? You have a man your own age across the road who would die for you, and you choose him, sure he's near as old as me. Have you had a look at yourself? You've been in magazines and catwalks, you're beautiful! Now I find out you're with an aul Yank that thinks he's James Bond and he's making a whore out of my daughter, and you let her Heather!"

Heather's face turned red with anger and disgust at what he had just said. She marched over to him, "Don't you ever say that word in this house again, especially to your daughter! And don't you dare insinuate that I allowed this to happen."

Esther had never seen them argue like that, and she felt so guilty, but she had told them the truth. "I'm sorry, I can't stop loving him! I've never loved Stephen. I knew this would hurt you both, but I can't help the way I feel. I wish I could have a normal life like Ruthann or Katrina, but I can't! I knew the moment I saw him, Dad, and I knew he fell in love with me too. It's never been easy. I feel empty without him, and right now I just want the world to stop so that I can get off! I've let everyone down. I'm a stupid failure."

There was silence. Joey sat down on the chair doing his best to calm down leaving Heather to have her say, "I've watched you work so hard, Esther. Up at 6 am, saving every penny you earned for Queenies and you made a success of it. Don't you ever say you're a stupid failure again. It was really hard not talking to you about Rueben, but my loyalty is with your father. I wanted Rueben to disappear out of your life, and I thought he had, but now he's back, buying castles with Marianne Stellabrass and causing havoc in this house."

"And that's why I'm leaving," Esther cried. "I can't stay here and watch him with her. He wanted to marry me, but we all know I can't!"

Joey couldn't believe what he was hearing. "He wants to marry you. Over my dead body!"

Esther was in turmoil, "I'm telling you this so that you understand he's not using me, Dad. Oh, what's the point? I'm sure you're both happy I'm leaving tomorrow."

She ran to the hall door, but Joey had more to say on the matter, "Have you ever thought what being married to him would be like? A young woman with an aul man sitting in the corner. You'd regret it in no time. You think I don't know, Esther, but I do. I know how a man thinks."

She looked at him knowing he really hadn't a clue how she felt, and as she went to run up the stairs, she stopped, and trying hard to stop crying, managed to reply, "I'm a woman, Dad and I know how a woman feels. But you just don't get it! Either of you." And she ran upstairs to bed.

This was the hardest thing she had ever had to do. Her love for Rueben just made everyone miserable and even though he was now with Marianne, she knew deep down that he could never love anyone else but her, they just couldn't be together and that was that. It was hard submitting to the truth, but it was necessary.

Downstairs, the discussion continued as Joey and Heather reconciled and came to the same conclusion, that it was for the best Esther leaving for London. Joey was convinced that by the time she got back, Rueben would be gone, and she would have found someone new. Heather, on the other hand, was not entirely convinced.

"She'll be alright, Heather. There's a touch of her mother in her and that's a good thing," he said with a little laugh.

The truth was out now and the release of it made Heather realise that it had been more of a burden on her than she had thought. Keeping that from Joey never felt right and she promised him she would never keep anything from him again, putting her arms around him to reassure him, very grateful that they were back on track.

"I love you, Mr O," she murmured in his ear, and he responded with a kiss on the cheek and,

"I love you too, Mrs O," then the security light started flashing.

"Ack no, that security light is flashing again, Joey. There's something wrong with it. Mosey tried to fix it earlier."

"I'll have a look now. Where is Mosey?" he asked.

"He was over at Ruthann's, although that might be him back now. He'll be wanting his dinner. I better get him something quick," and she let go of Joey making her way over to the fridge briskly.

Joey opened the back door and there was a loud bang! He fell to the ground. Heather watched helplessly and screamed.

Twelve

Esther sprinted down the stairs to the horrific sight before her. Her poor distraught mother lunged over her father, screeching, "Joey! Please, No, Joey!" There was blood everywhere. "Ring the ambulance!"

Esther managed to ring the ambulance in her state of distress, and within minutes police, ambulance and even the neighbours made their way speedily to see what had happened. The journalists who lived locally in the Dungiven area hurried over with their camera crew to catch the breaking news first-hand. Joey was taken to the hospital straightaway with Heather faithfully by his side but emotionally disturbed. It was mayhem, but he was still alive and that was the main thing. Their home was now officially a crime scene, and investigations were underway with forensics all around the cottage.

Esther, John and Stephen tried to deal with the immediate aftermath until Ruthann and Mosey got there, bursting through the carnage, frantic at the reality of what had just happened. John and Mosey exited as quickly as they could to get over to the hospital. It was a long and brutal night, but the adrenaline and trauma kept them going.

It was the early hours of the morning before everything quietened down. Esther had answered so many questions from the police. She was now emotionally and physically drained. There had been numerous phone calls until two o'clock in the morning. Ruthann and Esther were both traumatised and waited with bated breath for the unwanted call from the hospital. All the chaos settled, and no news was good news until the telephone rang. They looked at each other perplexed. It could only be the hospital. Esther answered it nervously, "Hello?"

"Esther, it's me, Rueben. I had to call you. I can't believe what I've heard. Are you alright? How I want to be with you, darling!"

Esther held the phone and closed her eyes, tears streaming down her face. She could hear his voice quivering, but she couldn't speak.

"Esther! Esther! Speak to me. I know you're there! Please answer me. I'm so sorry to hear about your father. I need to see you; I love you my darling."

Esther apprehensively set the phone down slowly and sat for a moment quietly sobbing, forgetting that Ruthann was listening and thought it was the hospital with bad news. "Please NO! don't tell me he's dead!" she cried.

This alerted Esther back to the nightmare. "It wasn't the hospital, Ruthann!"

"Who was it?" she asked mystified.

"It doesn't matter. I need to lie down and so do you. Let's try and get some rest."

They got very little rest and got up again at 6 am, thoughts of the night before taking complete possession of their minds as they tried to understand it all but couldn't. They eventually arrived at the hospital. Heather, John and Mosey were all in the waiting room, all exhausted. Heather appeared very pale just glaring at the floor, even the presence of Ruthann and Esther didn't move her.

Ruthann broke the dismal atmosphere, "How is he?"

Heather looked at John. "You tell her, John."

He updated them that the medical team had removed the bullet but then they were concerned about the bleeding but now they had managed to get that stopped.

"Oh, thank God!" raved Ruthann.

"Don't get too excited, he's in ICU, on a ventilator. We are not out of the woods yet." John went on to explain that fortunately for Joey, the bullet had hit him on the shoulder. The police said a handgun was used and that they had all been interviewed at the hospital. While they talked, Esther was concerned about the sheer exhaustion on her mother's face.

"Why don't you go home and get some rest, Mum? I'll stay here," she said kneeling down beside her and holding her hand.

Heather raised her head and glared angrily at Esther, pushing her hand away. "He's my husband and I'm staying here. Anyway, you have a plane to catch so you had better go!"

They all looked at one another in absolute confusion at Heather's reaction. How could she think that Esther was going to leave for London now, under those circumstances? Alarmed by this Esther quickly stood up, baffled by her mother's words but thinking maybe she misunderstood.

"What are you talking about, Mum? Surely you don't think I'm going to leave now?"

Heather stood up beside her with a look that Esther had never seen before. "We would all be better off if you did, so go! You do nothing but cause trouble when you're here!"

John was aghast at Heather's inexplicable statement and smoothly declared, "Come on now, Heather, you can't be saying that now, Esther's upset too."

But Heather was adamant. She had about as much as she could take from Esther and assumed a lot of this was her doing. "I nearly lost my Joey because of her selfishness." And she stared angrily at her, "You and your Yankee Commander!"

This was totally out of character for Heather, everyone was speechless. They had never heard her speak to anyone like that before let alone her daughter.

"But I hadn't been seeing him, Mum. You know that!" Esther blurted with desperation.

"You liar! You did, I saw you! I can see everything from the kitchen window, and I saw him carry you into his Land Rover, driving you up to that base. Are you telling me I didn't? I could never have told your father. I've lied to him so many times because of you, and now he's at death's door!"

Everyone was quiet, shocked by this proclamation. Mosey glanced at Esther and shook his head in shame at her. "How could you, Esther?" he said.

But Ruthann was in disbelief and had heard enough. "Hold on a minute! Esther loving Rueben had NOTHING at all to do with Daddy getting shot. How could you, Mummy?"

Heather, acting strangely and ignoring Ruthann, moved towards Esther as if she was about to hit her. All of them felt the volatile atmosphere, it was like she had been possessed. John stood up quickly, astonished by what was happening and wanted to at least try and clear the air. He may not have agreed with Esther's love life, but she certainly didn't deserve her mother's wrath, not at this tragic time! But Heather proceeded to add to her hate-speech,

"There's bombings and shootings and riots everywhere! But you thought the threat on your father's life wasn't that SERIOUS?" she shouted.

John had to quickly grab Heather by the arms to try and calm her down in case any of the medics heard and they would be asked to leave.

"Please, Mummy, let me explain, please," Esther begged her mum, bringing tears of compassion to Ruthann, but Heather remained so hard-hearted it was like she had become a different person, and she kept on shouting.

"I've heard you explain over and over again. You love him! I'm fed up hearing it. It's always about you, Esther! Now you go home get your bags and get out of my sight!"

Esther stood rigid, weak with brokenness. It was plain to see her mother hated her. How could this be fair? She needed Rueben so much right now, but she couldn't have him. She needed her family, but she was the outcast. She needed love but instead got accusations of being the main factor in her father getting shot. It was all too much and her only option was to turn on her heels and run and that's exactly what she did. Ruthann ran after her, trying to urge her back, yelling that their Mum didn't mean it, but as far as Esther was concerned, she meant it alright, and it was time for her to go!

It all quietened down, and the doctor finally marched up the corridor to speak with them. He told them Joey was off the critical list and that they were pleased with his progress. That was such a relief to them all, so they decided to go home and get some rest. The doctor allowed them to see Joey briefly, but Heather found it all too disturbing, even with the good news. "Nothing is ever going to be the same again," she whispered to herself.

When they got back to the cottage, Sandy was there. She put the kettle on to make tea for everyone and had the place clean and tidy so that they all could relax.

"Thank you, Sandy. You've been a great help to us," Ruthann said, observing how spotless the kitchen was. "Is Esther here?"

Sandy tried to answer but was overcome with tears. Heather looked at her with her cold-as-ice expression and asked, "What's happened? What has she done now?"

Ruthann rolled her eyes, having sympathy for her mother but not excusing her behaviour. Mosey took Sandy by the arm and pulled the chair out from under the table for her to sit down. She pointed to the letter propped up on the fruit bowl. Ruthann gazed at it and got a strange shiver down her spine before then hesitantly opened it and read,

"Oh no! I'm so sorry, Sandy."

Sandy kept on sobbing.

"What does it say, Ruthann?" Mosey was getting impatient.

"It's from Esther. She's gone, and Stephen has gone with her!"

Heather sat down and began to breathe louder as if she was having a panic attack, so Ruthann hurriedly got her a glass of water. Mosey caringly put his arm around Sandy but John couldn't keep his anger in. "He never even told me. What's he away for? When's he coming back? I need him at the farm!"

Sandy replied sobbing, "I don't know, John. Esther needed him too. He's always been honest with me about his feelings towards her, so, he's gone with her."

"Even so, Sandy," said Ruthann, perplexed by it all, "This must be very hard for you."

Sandy hung her head in sorrow but answered Ruthann, "Yes of course, but the main thing is that Mr O'Donnell is going to be alright."

Over at the Castle, Rueben paced up and down his office completely distraught thinking of Esther, questioning if he could have dealt with things any better, or if had he lost her forever. His heart was yearning for her, he needed her so much but there was nothing he could do. He felt helpless, and he hated that feeling, he was always able to find the answers and make the right decisions but not with this heart-wrenching conundrum. He grabbed his coat but as he was about to leave, Marianne came parading in.

"You left the door opened sweetie? You must be waiting on someone, but it can't be Esther because she's gone."

He looked at her with indignation. "What do you mean she's gone? She can't have, her father's just been shot. Esther wouldn't leave her family at a time like this!"

Marianne sniggered quietly loving the fact that she knew more than him. "She's gone to London."

Rueben turned to her and asked suspiciously, "How do you know all this?"

She smiled condescendingly at him. "Oh, I'm a bit like you, Rueben. If I need to know something, I'll get my answers one way or another."

"I can assure you, Marianne, you are nothing like me."

She strutted over to him and put her arms around his shoulders, relishing her power to impart this classified information to him. "Your little piece of forbidden fruit has done a runner, Commander!"

He grabbed her arms and pushed her away. "You're enjoying this aren't you?"

She laughed. "Oh no, Commander, it's breaking my heart," she replied sarcastically. "But I have one more piece of information that might break yours, Stephen McCarthy has gone with her!" And with that she smugly paraded back out through the door, smiling.

"I'll do my own investigations, thank you!"

She shrieked back, "You do that, but I think you'll find I'm right!"

Rueben went straight to the drinks cabinet and poured himself a brandy, drinking it neat, then packed a bag and left suddenly. No one knew where he went or how long for, although he was needed back at the naval base and arrived back two days later. In that time, Marianne seemed to have had a personality transplant doing all she could to make him feel wanted, which made him feel uneasy. Everything was going according to her plan. Esther had gone and that left Rueben alone for her to ensnare him like a fly in a spider's web.

She had obviously been using his office while he was away, as there was a nail file and nail varnish sitting on a magazine on the coffee table. He recognised the face on the front cover of the magazine. It was Esther looking right at him. He snatched the magazine, gazing at her agonizingly, "Damn you Esther! Why didn't you marry me?"

Thirteen

A few days before Joey was due to be discharged from the hospital, Heather received an urgent call to say that he had suffered a massive stroke. Not only had it affected his speech, but he was also unable to walk. After months in the rehabilitation ward, they could see that Joey wasn't getting any better and resigned him to a wheelchair. The medical team did everything they could, but Joey began to deteriorate rapidly and had now become virtually unrecognizable. It was like the life had been sucked out of him since the shooting. Heather cared for him as best she could with the help of a nurse who called her every morning but was just so grateful that he was alive. She blamed the stress of the shooting as the main factor for his stroke, but with the help of Mosey, made the front room into a bedroom for him so that friends could come in and chat with him. Tommy and Rita were regulars and of course, the Reverend Stewart. Mosey kept the business going as best he could while Sandy had become a great asset to the household, helping as much as she could with the cooking and cleaning.

Unfortunately for Uncle John, he had to take on the extra work at the farm after Stephen left, and that had a seriously negative impact on his courtship with Eileen, so she ended the romance accusing him of neglecting her. In all this time no one heard anything from Esther or Stephen, but Heather stealthily bought the magazines Esther featured in as she missed her so much. Rarely was her name mentioned at the cottage, but she was very much in everyone's thoughts. Life for all at the cottage had changed considerably. It had taken Heather weeks to get into a routine with Joey at home but eventually she did, and even though it was difficult, she never once complained.

It was Tuesday morning; the day Ruthann came to visit with Thomas. Heather was always glad to see her as Ruthann's presence made life feel a tad normal again just for that short time, and Joey always smiled when he saw Thomas. Ruthann carried Thomas in from the car and laid him down on the chair to sleep while Heather made the tea. She noticed how tired and depressed her mum was and wondered how long she could keep going, knowing caring for her father was not an easy task.

"You look exhausted, Mum. You're a real trooper!"

"It's my job! I have it to do. He's not going into a home it would kill him, and I couldn't bear it. For better for worse, in sickness and in health, those were my vows and I'm sticking to them. He would do the same for me. I know he would."

This brought the subject around very nicely to something Ruthann needed to tell her. "Speaking of vows, Mum. I have some news for you."

She looked at Ruthann horrified. The last thing she needed to hear right now was any more bad news, and she could see by the hesitant look on Ruthann's face she had something to say that she didn't want to tell her but had to.

"Vows? Please don't tell me your marriage is in trouble, Ruthann. Honestly, I just couldn't cope with that right now!"

There was nothing wrong with Ruthann's marriage, on the contrary, she couldn't be happier, so Heather's statement made the news she was about to disclose to her mum less complicated.

"No, Mum, of course there's nothing wrong with me and Robin. It's not that, it's just," she paused for a moment giving Heather even more reason to be anxious. "Okay, I'm just going to say it. Esther rang me."

Heather looked at her with excitement, a reaction that amazed Ruthann. Heather really needed to hear from Esther, and this was great news. Deep down she hoped Ruthann was going to add that she was coming home, but Ruthann had something completely and shockingly different to tell her.

"That's great news, Ruthann."

"Well, maybe this is good news too, Mum. Esther and Stephen got married," and again she paused. "They got married a few days after they left here."

This was like a bolt from the blue, even unbelievable to Heather. This wasn't good news; it was confusing news. Heather's reaction was to start fussing around the kitchen picking up the dish cloth and wiping down the surfaces until Ruthann took her by the shoulders and stopped her.

"You need to talk about this, Mum. You can't keep holding this emotion or whatever it is inside you any longer. Surely, you're not still blaming Esther for the IRA shooting Dad?"

Tears flowed down Heather's face. It was like the pain she had bottled up all this time had been released. "Of course, I'm not blaming her. I love her! She's my daughter, but why doesn't she come home?"

Ruthann hid her astonishment. She hadn't expected her to break down, this was her mother. But even though she felt empathy for her she still had to be honest.

"She needs to hear that from you, Mum, you need to tell her. Esther thinks you hate her and that it's all her fault, and honestly, I don't blame her after everything you said to her. Isn't it time you both started talking? Aren't you glad she married Stephen? After all, you and Dad wanted this for years. Is there nothing she can do that's right for you?"

Ruthann couldn't hold her temper any longer. The way her mother had dealt with Esther was vile and it was time she faced up to that. It was harsh being unable to mention her sister's name in case she upset her mother; it was inexplicable. The lie had been dormant for too long and it was time to remove it forever. Heather eventually sat down as if she had given in but she wasn't glad Esther had married Stephen, especially knowing justifiably that she didn't love him, always making it crystal clear she loved Rueben. So why marry Stephen?

"Am I really that bad?" she said miserably. It was like she was pleading with Ruthann to say no, but Ruthann had enough of her polite conversations.

"You've always been a great mother, loving and caring more than any of us could ask for, but you were really out of order with Esther, and you know it. You have to apologise to her, otherwise, this is it." She lifted her hands in the air walking around in a small circle, a little dramatically but only to ensure her mum was getting the message loud and clear. "Just because that happened, Dad didn't give you the right to condemn her and ex-communicate Esther! If loving someone is such a dreadful crime then we all need to go to prison, and for a very long time!"

Heather burst hysterically into tears. Ruthann was really firing those truth bombs, and they were hitting her hard.

"Oh, Mum, please don't cry like that. Please!" she pleaded, never having seen her mother so broken before.

"I'm a horrible mother. I don't know what came over me with Esther. I'll never forgive myself, Ruthann. I was so frightened Joey was going to die. I still am."

Stunned by her mum's confession but also relieved that she had finally succumbed to a truce, Ruthann was thankful that she was now sharing her worries instead of locking them up. She could see the release already on her face. The dark cloud was now leaving.

"You were in shock, Mum. It was the worst moment of your life! You can put all this behind you now if you would just talk to Esther."

Heather seemed in deep thought but still had questions she wanted answers to. "But why did she marry Stephen? Surely, she wouldn't marry him just to please me! Would she?"

Ruthann looked at her for a moment then said quietly and calmly, "Why don't you go over to London and ask her, Mum?"

She knew Ruthann was going to say that, and she also knew it was the only way forward. "But what about Joey? I can't leave Joey!"

"You can! We will all do our fair share here while you're away. It's the only way you're going to get this mess sorted! Besides the break will do you good!"

Ruthann missed Esther so much. She cried many times trying to hide her sadness from Robin, but he secretly observed her pain and without the necessary words, he comforted her. This was the breakthrough that was required and maybe now the family could move on together, but time was of the essence especially with Joey's health declining. Heather walked around the kitchen absorbed in thought while Ruthann reminisced on how she was always the strong, focused woman, but now so timid and frightened, struggling to make a decision, yet in the midst of it all there was a flicker of hope with her determination to take back what was rightfully hers.

"Do you have her address?" she piped up with her eyes wide open in enthusiasm.

This was the answer Ruthann had hoped for. She tried not to show how excited she was, but her heart was doing summersaults. "No, I don't, but she did say they lived in a flat near the agency, so if you go there first, they'll tell you."

"Alright. I'll go!"

"Oh, Mum, I'm so glad!" Ruthann couldn't contain herself and threw her arms around her. "You're doing the right thing!"

It didn't take Heather long to get everything sorted. It was a Friday, and she went into town to book her ticket with the travel agent while Sandy stayed with Joey. It was market day in Dungiven and it was busy. She thought she would nip over to the fruit and veg stall to get grapes as they were Joey's favourite. As she went to cross the road, a car slowed down and pulled up beside her. Heather stopped and looked in; it was Rueben. He wound down his window.

"Mrs O'Donnell, please listen. I'm not your enemy. My only crime is loving your daughter. I've only stopped to tell you how sorry I am to hear about your husband and everything you've been through. If there's anything I can do, please let me know."

He had taken her by surprise; he was the last person she expected to see today of all days and with that, she was confounded by what to say to him. He possessed a sad look of abandonment on his face that softened her heart. Although she certainly didn't feel as angry towards him as she used to, there was still the uneasiness. Their lives had changed, it took her a long time, but she had ultimately recognised his love for Esther. It was what he represented that she despised, still believing that having the presence of the US navy nearby was a threat to her family! But all this mess wasn't Rueben's fault, even though she had previously assumed it was. The country had also changed; belonging to a certain religion or culture, even having an unpopular surname could be deemed as offensive to paramilitary organisations who now seemed to have more power than the government.

"I appreciate that, Rueben. It has been very hard for us all. I'm aware you love Esther and how much she loves you, but I have some bad news for you that you may not want to hear, but I feel you should know."

Rueben rammed in, "She married Stephen, I know," he said turning his head and rubbing his chin to distract her from the pain that was written all over his face.

Heather's shocked reaction caused her to raise her voice. "How on earth did you know that?"

"I followed her to London a day or two after she left with the intention of taking her back to New York to marry me and live there, but it was too late. I arrived a few hours after she had married Stephen." He shook his head, trying to hold back his tears but carried on. "She felt it was the right thing to do for the family and for your safety and blamed herself for all the pain she'd caused. I suppose it was her way of trying to make things right. She hoped that maybe one day we would all understand. I can tell you now, Mrs O'Donnell, I'll never understand! This all seems so damned unnecessary!" He looked at Heather and understood those tears in her eyes.

"I'm so sorry, I didn't know," she replied feeling weak from the reality of his words. "I'm going over to see her. We haven't spoken in all this time; they need to come home. I don't know what to say, Rueben, it's all such a mess and it's all my fault! I'm sorry, I really am. I need to go!"

She ran back in the direction she came. Rueben watched her through his rear-view mirror.

Fourteen

Heather arrived in London and made her way by taxi from the airport to the model agency that Esther was working for, or at least that's what she thought, but they informed her she hadn't worked for them in quite a while but gave her the address they had, explaining it wasn't that far to walk to. Heather presumed Esther may have had a better offer with another agency. The flat was a bit further than she had anticipated and her feet were starting to hurt, but eventually, she reached her destination. The main door of the building looked as if it had seen better days, in fact, the whole neighbourhood felt dicey, so Heather looked at the address again believing she must have got it wrong, but no, that was the right place. She knocked on the door and an old woman with a shawl around her opened it and asked who she was looking for. Heather explained while looking down the pokey hallway, alarmed at how dingy the place was.

"First floor on the left," and she shuffled on down the dreary hall and disappeared into a room.

Heather reluctantly crept up the creaky stairs. There was a strong smell of stale cigarette smoke and damp, all rolled into one and it was dark. The greenish-brown wallpaper peeling off the walls didn't help; it had obviously seen much brighter days. There was the sound of a man and a woman arguing in one of the rooms on the ground floor, along with some kind of weird hippie music coming from another room on the first floor. Surely this can't be where they live, she thought. The creaks continued until she got to the designated flat or bedsit as it had now revealed itself to be. She knocked on the door and noticed the handle was about to fall off and considered how unsafe the place was. It all seemed very strange. Heather had convinced herself the agency had given her the wrong address until the door opened and there stood Esther.

"Mum! What are you doing here?"

They were both shocked but for different reasons.

"I could ask you the same question, Esther, but right now I'm just so happy to see you!"

Esther froze to the spot completely amazed that her mother had made the effort to come and see her.

"So, can I come in?"

"Yes, but I warn you, you will be shocked."

She was right. Esther led her mother into an equally unpleasant room.

"Why are you and Stephen living here, Esther? Surely you can afford better than this, working as a model in London, and with Stephen working too. I expected something a lot posher!"

There was a sink and a free-standing cabinet with a two-ring cooker sitting on it, two wooden chairs and a small table, and in the corner behind the door was a grey two-seater settee with vintage stains on it. It was dark with only one small window veiled with a torn net curtain. It all felt very claustrophobic.

"Stephen is the only one working and renting in London is really very expensive, but why are you here Mum?"

"I've come to apologise to you, Esther. I was so unkind to you. I didn't mean to say those awful things to you, my head was all over the place. Please forgive me, I miss you so much, love, and so does your father. He can't express how he's feeling but I know when he looks around the room, he's looking for you." Heather moved closer to Esther to hold her, but she pulled away.

"Don't, please. We've all been through a lot; I miss Dad too. I didn't think I was ever going to see any of you again. Did you tell Daddy I married Stephen?"

"I did," said Heather, trying hard to digest the gloomy surroundings her daughter lived in. "It made him very happy, but not me! Why did you marry him, Esther, you never loved him. Why?"

Esther couldn't believe what she was hearing. After all the years of listening to her raving on about how great a person he was and how he was the only one for her, had she changed her mind? But she was right, even though she had married Stephen, she still didn't love him.

"Circumstances! You know what it's like to be rejected, you did the same thing to me. So, in answer to your question, I had no choice!"

It felt like a no-win situation for Heather. She knew Esther was referring to her family rejecting her because of Joey, but Esther marrying Stephen because she felt rejected was something she couldn't fathom.

"I don't understand, what do you mean?"

Esther knew she didn't understand so it was time to explain, but without words. "Follow me then."

Heather followed Esther into a small room connected through a doorway. It was pokey and dark with the curtains closed. There was only a bed and a wardrobe, but Esther led her to the other side of the bed where on the floor was a cot with a tiny baby in it.

"That's why!"

Heather looked at the baby and looked at Esther. "Are you babysitting for someone?"

"No, Mum, that's your granddaughter!"

Heather was dumbfounded. You could see by her expression that she was trying to work it out. "My granddaughter?"

"Yes! Your granddaughter!" Esther sat down on the side of the bed while Heather stared at the baby. "She has Downs Syndrome, Mum; it's to do with her chromosomes."

Heather touched her very small delicate hand. "I know what Downs Syndrome is. I read about it in a booklet at the hospital." This was overwhelming. "My granddaughter. She's beautiful Esther."

Esther could see Heather's lips trembling, trying to hold back the tears and stay strong, but Esther knew that what she was about to say next would make those tears flow faster than a river.

"There's more, Mum. She has leukaemia and she has to go back into hospital, and we've been told she won't be coming home ever again."

This was more than a nightmare. Heather never thought she'd be facing something like this with her children. Right now, all she wanted to do was to phone Joey and tell him the news, so that he could tell her what to do, but not even this was an option now. Suddenly, she felt so alone and without the answers she needed to give her devastated daughter.

"NO! This is terrible, Esther," was the only reply she had.

"I know, Mum," said Esther calmly.

Heather unleashed those tears, weeping uncontrollably, trying to say something. Esther didn't need to hear what she said, she knew exactly what the next question would be.

"Margot Heather McCarthy. After you and Margot Fonteyn, the famous ballerina. I always thought if I had a daughter she would go to ballet school, but that won't be happening now."

Heather put her arms around her, knowing as a mother she needed that embrace more than anything right now, and this time Esther accepted it.

"When was Margot born?"

"The seventh of August."

She put her head down on Heather's shoulder like it was a sign of surrender and her help was needed. Heather felt it.

"Oh, Esther how could you go through all this on your own?"

Esther lifted her head quickly and stared at her perplexed by the remark.

"But I'm not on my own? I have Stephen! He's been a fantastic father. I couldn't be this strong without him."

Heather squeezed her hand tightly. "I knew you would make a fantastic mother; you're stronger than I could ever have imagined." Esther shook her head feeling unworthy of the praise. "And that's just what I would expect from Stephen, except he's not the father is he?"

That was like a full-blown punch hitting Esther on the most delicate part of her gut when she was least expecting it. "No, he's not, but I expect you know who is."

It took a minute for Heather to absorb all that information. She drew a deep breath and continued, "I know that Rueben doesn't know he's the father because I was talking to him a few days ago. He said he'd been over to see you, but you had just married Stephen. Why didn't you tell him you were pregnant?"

Esther jumped up off the bed and the mood changed quickly. She was about to spill her pain out, but now, astonished at just how insensitive her mother was by asking her that, after everything she had been through, wasn't it obvious?

"Why do you think I didn't tell him? I can't believe you're even asking me that! Can you imagine what would have happened if I had told him? It would have broken his heart even more than it is already. As for my heart, it's been smashed so many times I don't think there's anything left. I'm so tired of crying. Now I'm losing my baby too. I don't know how much more I can take."

She lifted her sleeve and wiped her eyes as she let go of that pain, but there was more she wanted to say. "And yes, Stephen knows everything. I told him I was pregnant the day we left. I didn't ask him to come with me, he insisted. He has stood by me so much, yet every day I feel so damn guilty that I don't love him!"

There was anger and fear in her voice and more tears. "Do you think it was easy for me to tell Rueben I had just married Stephen, knowing I was carrying his child? Knowing the only one I ever wanted to have in my life was him? Knowing that I couldn't put my family through any more. Do you think I wanted to live here in this dump with my dying daughter when I could have been living in a New York apartment with the man I adore and Margot's real father, sharing the pain with him? No Mum! But I had no choice! And right now, I feel like I've let everyone down, again, even my wee daughter!"

The strength drained from Heather as she listened. She realised it wasn't Esther who let everyone down, it was her! It was only now she could see that her daughter was the strong, caring, faithful one who gave up so much, while she on the other hand only cared what people would say, hiding safely behind the misconception of being the devoted wife and mother she had always likened herself to be. Yet here was Esther, the one who truthfully stood firm in her responsibilities and loyalties to others, even in the toughest of times.

She quickly reflected back to the night that she and Joey ran off to get married, throwing caution to the wind regardless of what anyone else had to say. Esther would never have done that, she was the real heroine, not her. This was a humbling moment for Heather, and it emphasized what Rueben had said was right – "It all seemed so damned unnecessary!" There was nothing they could have done to prevent Joey from that gunshot subsequently leading to his stroke! Heather now understood that it was Esther who bore the brunt of it all, just as much if not more than she had.

"Oh, Esther! You haven't let anyone down, I have. You're beautiful inside and out. Of course, I understand. This is all so terrible! You have as much right to love as anyone. This is all my fault! Not yours."

Even though the tears flowed from both of them, there was also a sense of healing, a healing that could only come from a mutual submission of all the mistakes and heartache from the past. It was time for truth and kindness and Esther wanted her mother to know everything, and this was the right time, no more pretending. She began,

"That day Rueben brought me up to Benbradagh was the last day I was with him, and you know I hadn't seen him in over a year, my heart was in bits. It was the happiest and saddest day of my life. Rueben proposed and gave me a beautiful diamond engagement ring, he said we'd never be separated again. Then I told him that we couldn't marry because of the death threat on Daddy's life. He was shocked by everything I told him. It hurt him so much, Mum, but I thought that if he was still based at Benbradagh it would be alright because I would still get glimpses of him around town; I needed that so much. I know that he bought the castle with Marianne just to be near me, but I stupidly thought he was having an affair with her. She wanted me to believe that and I fell for it. On the very day Stephen and I got married, he arrived. I couldn't believe it and again I had to let him go. It was like I'd stuck a dagger in his heart, and mine. If only he'd got there three hours before, I would have gone with him. I'd made those vows and that was that. I guess it just wasn't meant to be, but when I watched him go, everything within me wanted to run after him and tell him I was going to have his child and that I could never love anyone but him. It was an awful day when it should have been the best. I regret it with all my heart. So, there it is. I went from being the most envied and successful woman in Northern Ireland to being the most unfortunate failure in London, making all the wrong choices after Katrina warned me, it was like she knew Rueben would hate me for the rest of my life, but I have Margot to think of now. She comes first!"

So that was it. Silence fell as they both contemplated everything that was said. The only sound there was, was the tiniest whimper from Margot. They both sat on the edge of the bed and watched her move her tiny delicate body in distress. Esther lifted her out of the cot and gave her some medication while weeping.

"Thank you for telling me all that, Esther. This really is a sad situation, but I want to help. We've got to put all that behind us now and start afresh. Why don't you, Stephen and Margot come home with me today? I'll ring the hospital and we'll get Margot transferred. I'll pay what you owe here, and ring Ruthann and she can get the bed made up for you and Stephen in your old room. You need support love, not judgement and I'm standing by you from here on in!"

A very astonished Esther immediately took the suitcase down from the top of the wardrobe but hesitated. "Mum, I don't want anyone to know that Margot isn't Stephen's."

Heather grabbed her arm and gave her that motherly look that Esther hadn't seen in such a long time, and replied, "No one will ever hear it from me. Now, is there a phone downstairs?"

"Yes," and she smiled at her mum.

"Thank you for forgiving me, love."

Fifteen

Heather explained everything to Ruthann so that she would know exactly what to do; after getting over the initial shock of the sad news that is, and true to her word, Heather spoke of Stephen being Margot's father. All the family were devastated. They couldn't quite understand why Stephen and Esther hadn't told them earlier but were thankful they were coming home. With all the information needed, Ruthann decided to organize a small family party for the homecoming with help from Sandy, although Sandy left speedily as she felt this was an inappropriate time to see Stephen, especially after finding out he was now a father.

From beds to cradles, sandwiches and cake, even Joey was looking spick-and-span in his new pyjamas, dressing gown and slippers, looking very relaxed in the big sofa-chair in the corner of the kitchen all ready for the momentous occasion. Robin brought his photography gear so he could capture the special moments, knowing how important that was. Uncle John asked to bring Stephen home on his own from the airport, as he wanted to talk to him privately. So, that left Mosey to collect Heather, Esther and Margot.

It was exciting for everyone to be together again at last, but the circumstances were tragic. They had seen to all the last-minute tasks like blowing up balloons and getting cocktail sausages into the oven. The scene was set. Ruthann had butterflies in her stomach thrilled she was going to see Esther again.

"I wonder what Uncle John wants to talk to Stephen about?" she said while setting the colourful serviettes on the table.

"I'm sure there's a lot for them to talk about," said Robin, "like why didn't he contact him or why did he leave? Anyway, it's none of our business, Ruthann, we'll just be there for them because I can't begin to imagine what they're going through right now. I'm only glad you got your mother to go over and see Esther when you did."

Robin set up his apparatus so that he could capture every heart-warming moment of the family together, as they knew it would be the first and last time with Margot, maybe even Joey. They heard Mosey's car turning into the drive, the horn beeping vigorously to let them know they had arrived. Ruthann's teary-eyed expression was a mixture of happiness and sadness, fear and hope. The car boot banged, the back door opened and Mosey led the way for Esther carrying Margot in her arms, wrapped in her pink baby blanket, with Heather right behind them. Ruthann ran over and carefully embraced them both.

"Welcome home, Esther. I'm so glad to see you. I've missed you so much, we all have."

Esther looked all around, and her eyes rested on Joey sitting in the corner and looking right at her.

"Oh, please let me hold my beautiful niece Margot, and you go see Daddy, he's looking at you," pleaded Ruthann.

Joey whimpered, aware of her presence. There was silence as Esther knelt down at his feet and saw the tears rolling down from his eyes. "Oh, Daddy, I've missed you so much. I'm so sorry I left but I had to! But I'm back now, and for good, with Stephen. We got married, Daddy just as you always wanted, and this is our little daughter, Margot. Meet your granddaughter."

Ruthann brought Margot over and gently held her on Joey's lap. Joey tried so hard to talk but he couldn't, and with a combination of frustration and happiness, he cried instead. In fact, everyone did apart from Mosey who quickly made the excuse of bringing in the rest of the luggage, effecting quite a getaway to avoid this very sensitive situation. It was such a moving occasion and Robin did capture every precious moment perfectly with his camera. It wasn't long before Uncle John and Stephen arrived back in time to see Thomas and Margot lying side by side for a photo and another with Esther and Ruthann holding their children.

Ruthann began to sing: "You are my sunshine, my only sunshine," and everyone joined in with, "You make me happy when skies are grey."

Joey whimpered loudly trying to sing while the tears just poured down Heather's face, who at this stage was sitting at his feet with her arms wrapped around his legs and her head on his lap. He relaxed his hand on her head as they all sang, "You'll never know dear; how much I love you. Please don't take my sunshine away."

It was the last time they would all be together. Early the next morning, Margot was admitted to Altnagelvin hospital in Londonderry. Stephen and Esther stayed by her side, doing everything they could to make this last part of her life as comfortable as possible. They dressed the room with teddies and dolls that the family had bought her. There was no time for anything else, being with Margot was the priority.

"Would you like something from the shop, Esther? I could get you a coffee or something?" asked an exhausted Stephen.

"No, I'm fine. Mum's coming anyway and she'll have a flask and sandwiches, that will do me. You go on ahead and get some air as well, you look shattered."

Stephen agreed and left while Esther curled up on the hospital chair beside the bed. She felt her eyes getting heavier and heavier and just as she was about to fall asleep, the door opened, and thinking it was Heather, she just kept on resting until she heard that voice.

"Hello, my beautiful daughter."

It was Rueben! Esther immediately jumped to her feet. "Rueben? What are you doing here?"

"I'm here to see my daughter. Why didn't you tell me, Esther? I hope Stephen knows he's not the father, is that why you married him? And tell me this, what have I ever done that was so bad, that you could do this to me? You must hate me!"

Esther was in shock at his presence but it comforted her to see him standing there, even though it was blatantly obvious he was furious with her, she was much too tired to argue and this was neither the time nor the place to debate who had done what. Yet even with her absolute exhaustion from everything, she found the strength to reply, boldly,

"Yes, Rueben you're the father! Yes, that's why I married Stephen and yes, he knows he's not Margot's father. No, I don't hate you. Yes, I love you so much the pain has gone numb! So, there you have it. I've dealt with everything wrong because that's what I do best, isn't it? It's all my stupid fault, but believe me, there's been a high price for every stupid mistake I've made. But now it's all about

Margot, as I'm sure you've also been informed, she is terminally ill, and time is precious. It's not about you or me, so please understand why I can't use what's left of my energy to fight or argue with you today."

Rueben stood speechless, observing her exhaustion. He had never seen Esther like this before. She was lost, confused and her physical appearance was emaciated, but yet so strong.

"I'm sorry I messed it all up," she said and turned her back on him, holding her hands up to her face.

He moved closer, longing to hold her in his arms, distraught that she was crumbling right before his eyes. He lifted his arm to pull her to him, but without noticing his act of compassion, she quickly turned back,
"Her name is Margot Heather McCarthy."

He immediately pulled his arm back and glared at her with disgust. His empathetic approach had gone now that she had used Stephen's surname. The horror that appeared on his face said it all. She realised what she had said but it was too late.

"No!" he demanded. "Her name is Margot Heather Redpath and don't you ever forget that!"

She stood rigidly, watching him looking down at Margot and holding her tiny little hand.

"I'm your father, darling. I love you and only wish we could have spent more time together. You'll meet your brother, Robert soon. Tell him I miss him. Do Widzenia, kochanie." (Goodbye my darling in Polish)

And with that, he walked out with tears streaming down his face. As he passed Stephen in the doorway, Rueben stopped and raged at him, "She is MY daughter, not yours!"

Stephen said nothing and just moved out of his way, leaving Esther startled by what he had just said. What did he mean by that? Who was Robert and why did he speak in that foreign language?

"I didn't tell him, Stephen, he already knew. He has ways and means of finding out everything, that's his job but I'm too tired to talk, I need sleep."

Stephen said nothing, just put a blanket over her as she fell onto the armchair completely worn-out.

As Rueben marched down the corridor, he met Heather walking towards Margot's room. They stopped and looked at one another. She could see how angry he was and knew immediately that he had found out Margot was his. She began to feel nervous and guilty.

"I know I'm the father, if that's what you're wondering Mrs O'Donnell. It's just a pity no one thought it important enough to tell me!" He marched on, but Heather called him back. He stopped and turned to her. "What?"

"Please keep this to yourself for Esther's sake."

He closed his eyes and shook his head. "You can be assured Mrs O'Donnell, I will keep your daughter's character intact!" He went to move off, but again Heather called him.

"What is now, Mrs O'Donnell?"

"I'm so sorry, Rueben. I really mean that."

He departed with Heather watching him until he disappeared around the corner.

Esther did get to sleep even though she was curled up on a hospital chair with just a blanket over her, but she was just too tired to care and went into such a deep sleep. It was like her whole body had switched off from everything, like someone had given her a handful of tranquillizers and she was floating peacefully on a cloud, a feeling she had never experienced before. Then she heard Stephen's voice shouting, "Esther! Esther, what's wrong with you? Please wake up."

It took her a few minutes to come round and then all of life's awfulness came flooding back to her, and more. She looked up and Heather stood crying at the cot with the nurse. She knew what had happened but had to hear it.

"I'm so sorry, love. Margot has died!"

The emptiness in her life was now that dark it was severe.

Margot's funeral was a sad and private affair. It was family only, but Rueben watched from afar. Esther knew he was there as he had just as much right as anyone else to be. How she longed for him to be beside her, just as much as he longed to be beside her; they needed each other so much it was cruel. She could feel his presence, and he could feel her pain. Ruthann grabbed Esther's hand but could see she was engrossed with something, so she turned to see what she was looking at; she was shocked and confused when she realised it was Rueben. What on earth was he doing there? But then he disappeared.

The sadness continued at the O'Donnell's home when another funeral took place two weeks later, as Joseph Patrick O'Donnell was laid to rest beside his granddaughter. The family were traumatised, and as the mourners dispersed, Heather and Esther were left by the graveside on their own, arms entwined around one another.

"Oh, Esther, one minute life is going so well, all the dreams and all the plans come together, then the next minute there's a tsunami that blows everything to pieces and you've got to put it all back together again, but with the main pieces missing."

"It's the same with the heart, Mum. But I don't think I can do it anymore. Life's too hard."

"We must Esther. We must take these pieces and make life work again. That's my faith, love, and that's what Joey and Margot would have wanted. We just have to!"

Sixteen

Six months passed slowly. The family grieved, especially Esther. She spent most of her time in bed holding Margot's pink blanket while Heather walked around the cottage troubled and upset, doing her best to deal with the aftershock of that tsunami that had hit her whole family. Stephen did everything he could to help Esther, but a lot of the time she seemed so lifeless that he became concerned she would never get better. However, he did go back to work for John even though it was a little awkward at first with Sandy, but she made it very plain to him that they would always be friends, and what happened was now in the past. It didn't matter to her anymore anyway as she had found someone else who made her very happy.

Now that Stephen was home and working for John, and after grovelling for days, John had got his relationship back on track with Eileen with the aid of a 9-carat gold engagement ring. Now they could start afresh.

Sadly, Rueben was quietly dealing with his own feelings, having only one other person he could confide in, Ralph. He and Katrina had been married for over a year now and were living in Arkansas, but they were both happy to help, even if it was only a listening ear at the other end of the phone. Rueben shared his pain about Margot and his love for Esther, but she was another man's wife and there was nothing he could do about that. There were also issues concerning his finances at the Castle, and with having fewer commitments at the naval base, he had begun questioning his life at Dungiven. Even though Marianne had become just about bearable to work with, as far as she was concerned Esther was out of the picture and she was now in with a chance, even though she wasn't. He wondered how long it would all last. They both understood there needed to be changes made at the Castle as the bills that were rolling in were substantial and they needed to get paid soon. So, Marianne decided to invest in some weekly entertainment and it being the mid-1970s, she thought discotheques were the best way to make money. Rueben hated the idea but gave in because he knew realistically it would help balance the books. So, the ballroom was replaced with flashing lights, mirror balls and a corner for the resident DJ to play his records on the turntable, naming it Young Hearts Nightclub. It not only was the gossip of Dungiven but surrounding towns. Even the young people from Belfast and Derry flocked to it. Rueben was wary of this as he wanted to keep a low profile but suddenly the disco at the Castle was in every newspaper with Marianne happy to pose for every picture expressing how hard she worked at getting this fantastic idea of hers up and running.

It was now Springtime 1975, Esther's favourite time of the year. Flowers were budding and the evenings getting lighter and brighter, and with that, she felt herself getting stronger, helping a lot more with the chores around the house and going for long walks. Heather also got back into a routine and life at the cottage showed hope for the future.

It was Tuesday and as per her normal weekly routine, Ruthann was visiting. It was great when she came as her visits meant coffee, cake and chat time for the three ladies, while Mosey happily showed young Thomas the cars he was working on. He had kept the business going just as Joey had requested.

Esther was on her own in the kitchen mopping the floor when Stephen pounded through the back door.

"Mind your feet, Stephen," she warned him, "I've just mopped there."

But that was the last thing on Stephen's mind. "Esther," he said in a very commanding voice. "I've made a big decision today. Do you remember I told you the reason Uncle John wanted to collect me from the airport on his own was because he wanted us to have the field beside his house as a wedding gift?"

Esther hadn't a clue what he was talking about. She didn't remember at all, but she could see how excited he was right now and didn't want to hurt him.

"Yes," she said, trying hard to be interested.

"Well, you'll never guess, it's now got planning permission on it, so I rang Paul, the architect guy I know, and he wants me to go over and have a talk with him about our plans. Do you want to come with me?"

Esther stared blankly out of the window knowing in her heart she didn't have any interest in this but was careful not to discourage Stephen in any way as she knew this was his dream. She turned to smile at him, but Stephen knew her well enough to know she wasn't interested but kept trying anyway.

"Would you like a veranda? You could sit out there with Ruthann and look up to the mountain, and we'll even get one of those swing seats! I know you'd like that."

Esther gave in and set the mop down. She slowly walked over to him lifting her arms to hold him. This was not at all what he expected, but he was over the moon with this spontaneous reaction. Looking at him lovingly, she said gently,

"Stephen McCarthy, you must be the kindest, loveliest man I have ever known apart from Daddy."

He smiled the biggest smile. It was a long time since he received a compliment like that from Esther. "I love you, Mrs McCarthy!" He awaited her reply, but there was none. "You still don't love me, Esther?"

"Oh, Stephen, you're the best friend a girl could have. Marriages can work based on friendship you know!"

She could feel how deflated he was with her answer, and again she hated herself for it but couldn't pretend. He headed out the door and she called out to him. He turned hoping that just maybe she was going to say she loved him.

"I'd love a veranda."

He didn't reply just tutted something and went out. Esther lifted her handbag that was sitting on the chair and took out a small box. She opened it and slipped the diamond ring on her finger holding it to her heart, then closed her eyes and stayed that way for a few moments. It gave her a sense of peace and calm until Ruthann bolted in with Thomas, shouting out for Uncle Mo.

"Are you alright Esther?"

She hadn't heard Ruthann pull up in the car. Ruthann sent Thomas out to see Mosey who had come bounding across the yard to meet him, lifting him up and swinging him around in his arms, eventually taking him over to see the cars. With that distraction, Esther quickly took the ring off and put it back in her bag.

"Oh yes. I'm fine. Really, I am."

Ruthann wasn't convinced but proceeded, "I was talking to Stephen there. He said he's going to see the architect about plans for the house. How exciting, but I think he would have liked it if you had gone with him."

"He'll be better at it without me Ruthann, this is his dream!"

"Not yours?" Ruthann probed.

"No, not mine but I'm grateful." She lifted the mop again and started mopping the floor.

"Robin and I wanted to know if you and Stephen would like to come with us to the Castle this Saturday night. Grandma Harvey is keeping Thomas overnight, so we thought we'd check out the new disco. I've heard great reports, although they have come from Marianne Stellabrass and she would say that."

Esther hated that name but tried not to show it. The very thought of that woman made her stomach churn, knowing the lies she had told in the past. Ruthann knew she despised her, so why did she even have to bring her name up?

"Have you been talking to her, Ruthann?"

"No, I have not. I wouldn't want to talk to her, mind you she's now saying she's getting married to Rueben. How true it is I don't know but she asked Ciara, the new girl I work with, if she would do her hair for it."

Esther tried hard not to show her emotions and continued mopping the floor.

"I thought it wouldn't bother you that much, especially after everything that you and Stephen have been through!" She said this with curiosity, but Esther gave nothing away too busy thinking over this invitation.

"So, Saturday night then. I'm sure Stephen would like to go out, so make it a yes from us."

"Great, right I'm going to get Thomas, so you get the kettle on. Mum's on her way over now, and I have a nice Victoria sponge in the car."

Esther smiled the biggest smile she had in a few years as Ruthann left.

"Right," she muttered to herself. "Time to shine!"

Stephen was glad they were all going out together. He felt slightly unsure about going to the Castle but chose to believe it was a good thing for their first outing as it might help Esther come to terms with Rueben and Marianne. He sat waiting in the kitchen with Heather while Esther was getting ready. It took her a while and the Harvey's had arrived. They beeped the horn and Stephen called Esther again. They heard the thud of her coming down the stairs, the door opened and in walked a very beautiful and sexy Mrs McCarthy in a tight short black sequined dress with black high heels. Her hair was long and flowing and her face was beautifully made up, but with a slight overload of red lipstick.

"Wow!" exclaimed a very proud husband. "Look at my gorgeous wife."

Heather looked but certainly did not get the same feeling Stephen was getting. She knew the effort was not for him.

"I'm ready," she said, and as she went to lift her bag she stumbled and then started to laugh.

Heather could smell the alcohol but ignored it, knowing Stephen hadn't picked up on it, because he was so engrossed with how attractive she looked. He knew she would turn heads; she always did but he was her husband, and she would be on his arm, and she did take his arm but only to keep her balance.

Seventeen

It was a busy night at the Castle and the carpark was full. You could hear the music blaring loudly from the reception with lots of people coming and going. It was a life that Esther had forgotten, or never really had a connection to, but tonight she had a purpose for this outing and nothing was going to ruin that. Ruthann was concerned for her, witnessing her erratic behaviour and wondered if the disco was something she wasn't ready for, but it was too late. Esther hobbled out of the car and staggered into the venue holding tightly to Stephen. Heads turned and elbows nudged, raising the alarm that the beautiful but complex Mrs McCarthy was making her way into Young Hearts Nightclub. A part of Esther enjoyed the attention, but no one could imagine the emotional pain she was in.

Robin found a small table at the back of the disco. Stephen grabbed Esther by the arm and led her through the crowd, and of course, as always Lizzy and Trish were propping up the bar, watching her every move.

"Well, would you look who's out tonight, Lizzie! Miss Magazine in all her style!"

Lizzie glared with envy. "Ack, would you look at the cut of her! She's not that pretty!"

"Aye, right Trish! And Paisleys a Catholic!"

Robin got the drinks in, and Esther knocked them back. It was her party and with great music, she couldn't help herself and started to dance. "Come on Ruthann, let's have a bit of fun. Come on and dance."

Ruthann was apprehensive but got up anyway and danced to save her sister's embarrassment as people were staring. Stephen made a face at Ruthann as if to say, what's going on? But Ruthann shrugged her shoulders while Esther kept up the show, looking all around as if she was trying to find someone but pretending to be having a great time, again the expert of pretence. The song finished and Ruthann dragged her by the arm to sit down. When she lifted Stephen's drink, he pulled it out of her hand.

"Haven't you had enough?"

"Oh, stop being an old fuddy-duddy!" and she threw her arms around him for a smooch. Stephen enjoyed this little chunk of affection, fully aware she had him wrapped around her little finger.

Once again, Ruthann watched another "Esther performance" but this one topped the lot as far as she was concerned. As she started to piece things together in her mind, she quickly came up with the right conclusion, Rueben!

"I'm just going to powder my nose!" Esther informed them as she released Stephen.

"I'll come with you, Esther," replied an adamant Ruthann, but this wasn't on Esther's agenda.

"I don't need chaperoning, Ruthann. I'll be back in a minute. Okay!"

She left them and made her way through a group of admirers who had only had the privilege of seeing the very gorgeous Mrs McCarthy in magazines and newspapers, but there she was in the flesh. They couldn't take their eyes off her, and she knew it. She swept her hair back from her face and as she walked past them, she accidentally rubbed shoulders with one of them, giving them ammunition to say what they were thinking.

"Look at that, Snowy! You wouldn't know what to do with that, sure you wouldn't!"

"I'd know alright!" he smirked, and they all laughed.

When they laughed even louder, it provoked Stephen to stand up making it known to them that he was her husband and he wasn't having her laughed at, but they just ignored him. Ruthann glared at him as if to say, go get her.

"There's nothing I can do, Ruthann. I know what she's like. If she's not back in ten minutes, I'll find her!" She could see he was bothered by it all but helpless.

Esther skurried up the corridor and past the ladies' toilets, just as Lizzie and Trish were walking out of them.

"Will you look, Lizzie, I wonder where she's off too, as if we didn't know!" with her Cheshire cat grin.

"Where?" Lizzie asked.

"Where do you think, you eejit? Mr Commander!"

"Never, and her a married woman!" smiling like the cat that got the cream.

Trish rolled her eyes, and they went back to the bar to broadcast the groundbreaking news.

Esther reached her destination which was Rueben's office and stood at the door straightening her dress, aware that it had crept up to an inappropriate height. She flicked her hair and as she was about to knock, she heard voices arguing, so she leaned toward the door to hear what was going on. The voices were getting louder,

"You had no right, Marianne! You have no idea how dangerous that is for me!"

"I'm a businesswoman; I must take risks!"

"So, stop involving me!" he shouted.

"You're a spineless coward!" she screeched back.

"Get out of my office now! You don't know me at all!"

Esther jumped back from the door and hid behind a tall green plant perched at the side. Marianne stormed out and raced down the corridor, oblivious to being watched. The door was left open and Esther sobering up fast, made her entrance while Rueben poured himself a brandy having no idea that he had a very special visitor.

"Trouble in paradise?" she said.

He turned quickly. "Esther! What are you doing here?"

"I needed to see you, but it's obviously a bad time."

She started to leave, knowing he wanted her to stay.

"No, please don't go. Come in. It's good to see you, but why? Are you alright?"

She took a deep breath and again fixed her dress, then walked boldly and confidently further into the room with his eyes permanently fixed on her.

"You need to listen to me, Rueben, but I don't have much time. I know you hate me for all I've done, but I need you to understand I had no choice."

Rueben seemed annoyed by this. The very thought that she actually believed he hated her was nonsense. "I don't hate you, Esther. I've tried my damnedest to, but I can't stop loving you! That's my problem."

Esther was so relieved to hear that and began to feel more comfortable, moving even closer to him and asking the question she needed to hear him answer. "So, why are you marrying her?"

Rueben laughed. "You still don't get it! I'm not marrying anyone, Esther! Is that what she's saying now? I wouldn't marry Marianne Stellabrass if she was the last woman on this earth."

That was a relief for her to hear him declare that. If only he knew the influence he still had on her life. As she looked into his dark eyes, she yearned to kiss him. He knew and moved closer to her, lifting her hand and kissing it. Again, he moved closer and kissed her neck. She responded, willingly.

"I know how much you've been through, my darling," he whispered. "I really wanted to be by your side." And he kissed her neck again. "I can't stop loving you."

Guilt came pouring over Esther like a flood. How she needed him in every way but couldn't, she knew it was wrong. "Don't, Rueben. I can't! I'm married to Stephen."

He jumped away so quickly, trying to save himself from his ceaseless longing for her, knowing he couldn't resist her, desperate that she belonged to another man.

"Damn it, Esther! Why are you here? I need you! I want to make love to you so much. But you're right, you do belong to Stephen!"

She didn't expect him to react like that, but she didn't know what she expected. It didn't matter right now anyway as she needed to tell him what he needed to know. "My heart will always belong to you, Rueben! And Stephen knows it. I'm here because I need you to know I still love you as much as I did the first time I saw you, but also," she hesitated, "Who is Robert?"

"No, Esther! No! I'm not doing this now because YOU feel you're ready to talk! This all needs to end. I can't go on like this. I can't be here anymore, it's killing me! Go to your husband; I'm going back to New York!"

She froze. He couldn't do this; her life just wouldn't be worth living. How could he say this? She cried the familiar pain and never-ending tears that had baited her life had made their way back again. "Please don't do this to me, Rueben! If you left, I would die, really I would! So many times, when I was in London, I wanted to ring you and tell you everything. I wanted you to be the first person to hold Margot, but I didn't feel I had the right to do that to you or my family, or Stephen! I never thought my baby was going to die, Rueben!"

He shouted back at her with all force, "Our baby! She was mine as well! Damn you, Esther! She was my daughter; you didn't let me be her father. You married Stephen! So don't act like you're the victim! I have feelings too!"

They had to let their pain out, a pain that had been festering for too long. Their hearts were breaking yet even through all their yearning for one another couldn't diminish, it just got stronger.

"This is not the end, Rueben. I can't live without you, and I know you feel the same. How could we forget that wonderful day on the mountain when we made Margot together? So, I messed up, I can only ask you to forgive me. Please Rueben!"

He calmed down and went to the drinks cabinet, pouring them both a brandy. "Of course, I've forgiven you. You're everything to me, Esther. You're all I have. Life can be one big pile of garbage, my darling. I'm pouring you a brandy, I never did get you that brandy in Renny's that rainy day, do you remember?"

How could she ever forget? They reminisced about that wonderful moment they had together but as he handed her the brandy, there was a knock at the door.

"Esther, are you there?" asked Stephen.

"Oh no! I must go!" She panicked, but he grabbed her arm.

"Please stay, Esther!"

She was tempted so tempted! Stephen yelled again. They looked at each other, neither of them knowing what would happen next! Until Rueben spoke up, "Okay, I'll make this easy for you," and he opened the door to a lost-looking Stephen. "Come in Stephen. Your wife is here."

Stephen stepped in reluctantly, looking crossly at Esther.

"I'm sorry, Stephen. I had to talk with Rueben."

The sadness returned to her face as her last attempt to make amends again fell right through her fingers. She needed Rueben to rescue her, not Stephen.

"Why didn't you tell me, Esther? I would have come with you. We were all worried about you. Let's go home now?"

She wavered and glanced at Rueben. He felt her reluctance to leave and gave her that look willing her to stay. The next few seconds were crucial and all three of them knew it. It was time for her to choose. Stephen looked at the floor, unable to do anything, powerless, knowing he may have lost this battle. Then suddenly, the choice was taken out of Esther's hands as Marianne pushed through and stormed up to her, glaring as if her next move was to punch her, but Rueben pulled her back.

"What's going on here?" she squealed like a woman possessed. "Do you mind? This is our home, and I think you and your husband should leave and head back to the fields where you belong!"

That was it, she knew she couldn't stay now, but this was the opportunity Esther had waited a long time for. She was fed up with Marianne's lies and derogatory remarks, so she threw her shoulders back, lifted her head high and glared right into her eyes.

"You know what, Marianne, you're nothing but a painted up, powdered up, outdated slapper and that blouse you bought from me would have looked better on a bulldog, the bulldog being a bitch too, only better looking. Now do yourself a favour and find a man that CAN stand you! If that's possible!"

Marianne raised her hand to hit her, but Rueben pulled her backwards while she screamed, "You cheeky cow!"

Stephen also took Esther by the arm, hauling her out through the door with Rueben watching. Esther quickly looked back and got a final glimpse of his sad face, knowing the opportunity had gone.

They got back to the cottage, the McCarthys having argued in the back seat the whole way home. The arguments and disputes progressed into the house. Heather, awakened by all the shouting, came down to see what was going on. Ruthann had now got involved and just couldn't understand how Esther could possibly want to see Rueben after everything she and Stephen had been through. Esther couldn't take anymore and decided to tell her.

"I'm fed up with secrets and lies! Rueben is Margot's father!"

Silence and shock fell on both Robin and Ruthann as they tried to digest this news, but Esther had started and now wanted them to know the rest.

"I had just found out for sure I was pregnant before I left for London. I had no idea what was going to happen with my contract, but I knew I had to go. Then when Dad was shot, I wanted to stay at home with Mum. Eventually, I would have told you all, of course. I know Rueben would have married me but us being together was dangerous for the family. I honestly thought he was moving on with Marianne in his life, I stupidly believed her."

Ruthann and Robin's mouths fell open in shock and horror at what they were hearing. Ruthann walked around in a circle, as everything became a lot clearer and began to make sense, even seeing Rueben at Margot's funeral. But Ruthann, sounding like mother, demanded answers.

"Did you know all this, Mum?"

"Yes," Heather timidly replied. "I knew from the minute I saw Margot."

An angry Ruthann stamped her foot on the floor frantically, distraught because no one trusted her enough to tell her. "I thought you could tell me anything. It was me you rang when you were in London, wanting to know about Dad! You could have told me then; I wouldn't have judged you. I would have helped you!" She sobbed feeling like she had been betrayed.

Robin went over and put his arms around her, understanding that she felt like the outcast when together they had only wanted to be there to help the family, but in return, they were lied to.

"When I think of Sandy crying and thinking you might have been unfaithful to her, Stephen. She was heartbroken when she heard about Margot and yet she helped out, cleaning the rooms for you coming home, such a lovely person, she didn't deserve that. Thankfully she's met someone else. I hope whoever he is, he treats her with the respect you didn't give her. You knew Esther loved Rueben or should I say - loves Rueben. You still do, don't you Esther?"

Esther paced to the back door to leave, unable to take anymore but Stephen stopped her. "No running away this time, Esther, you need to answer. I need to know!"

Esther pulled her arm away and screeched at the top of her voice, "You do know! You all know! Yes, I do I love him so much I could die right now! How much more do I have to give before I can live again!"

Stephen did know, but now she had made it very clear to him, it was his time to leave. "I've heard you, Esther, loud and clear! I've been there for you, I've loved you, but now I can't go on pretending that you just might grow to love me. I'm going to stay at John's until we can get things sorted out. If that means making our marriage work or divorcing, I don't know right now. Goodnight." He flung open the door nearly taking it off its hinges and left.

There was silence. Heather watched her fragile daughter so heartbroken and burned out, and how it was distressing everyone. It was better for her to have some time on her own. Esther picked up her shoes and bag from the floor to go to bed. It had been a disastrous night but at least now they all knew the truth. Before she left the room, she hung her head in sorrow and softly said,

"My life always had a strange way of drifting in the wrong direction without my authority!"

Eighteen

Stephen stayed at John's. He and Sandy talked a lot now that the truth was out. Sandy, naturally relieved at the revelation had sympathy for him because he looked so miserable all the time, albeit he noted how much happier she was. Sandy came through their break-up as best she could, reminding herself that he was a fool, infatuated with a woman who was very much in love with someone else and for her it had all worked out for the best. Stephen kept himself busy working on the foundations of the new house. He kept away from the cottage thinking it best to have a few days' break before their impending discussion about their future. He was nervous, unwilling for the marriage to end. He loved Esther, he had always loved her and could never see himself with anyone else. Sandy tried to advise him the best way she could, while John would give him a manly pat on the shoulder every now and then to let him know he was there for him. Both John and Mosey now knew that Rueben was Margot's real father but wisely said nothing. The only concern Stephen had was if John told Eileen because then the whole town would know, but John's word was his word.

It was nearly a week from the Castle episode, and Heather invited John, Eileen and Stephen over for dinner as Mosey wanted to speak to everyone. This was out of character for him, so they all wondered what on earth he could possibly want to say. It would be the first time Stephen and Esther would be in a room together since that night, apart from having glimpses of one another when outside. Stephen made a special effort to look his best while Esther didn't care at all. The week on her own had only confirmed her feelings and she could no longer live the lie. She hadn't made any effort in her appearance and shuffled downstairs in her house slippers and sat at the table, only glad to see the Harveys pull up, knowing it would help ease the tension with Stephen. Stephen arrived on his own without John and Eileen. Heather asked where they were.

"They'll be over shortly, I just wanted to give them a bit of time on their own, you know how it is," he said as he looked at Esther. She looked away and fiddled with her fork, noticing how nicely dressed the table was with serviettes and flowers as the centre piece.

"Go on over beside Esther, Stephen." Heather had everything and everyone organized. They could hear Mosey galivanting down the stairs and in he came looking very handsome in his new shirt and trousers, then came an overpowering waft of aftershave. Ruthann was the first to comment.

"My oh my, Mosey O'Donnell! It's only us, you don't have to impress us."

They all laughed, even Esther.

"Don't listen to them, Mosey," said Heather fascinated by his appearance; she hadn't seen her son so well-groomed in a long time. "Come over here and sit down beside me. You look very handsome."

Mosey sat down beside Heather as she explained to them all that John and Eileen would be over shortly.

"It's okay, Mum, they don't have to be here. They already know what I'm going to say to you all anyway."

They waited patiently to get this great mystery solved. Mosey rose to his feet as if about to make a speech.

"I just want to say I know this family has had its fair share of problems, to say the least, but sometimes through the problems you find things out about yourself that you didn't really know, and when you know that sort of stuff, then," he stopped to take a breath and wiped his brow with his hand, everyone waited enthusiastically. "And from that nice things can happen."

This didn't make the conundrum any easier and Robin could hold back no longer, bursting into laughter while Ruthann dug him in the arm not wanting Mosey to get distracted, as she knew only too well this was an extremely rare occurrence.

"Come on man, what's this about?"

"Okay, sorry. Well, the thing is," he said nervously. Nobody wanted to speak just in case they put him off what he had obviously rehearsed. "Oh, darn it. There's only one way to say this, I've got engaged. I'm getting married!"

Everyone was shocked at this announcement. It was the last thing they thought he would say.

"You what?" yelled Heather. "But I haven't met her. You've never even brought her here Mosey. Are you sure?" Another marital mistake was the last thing she needed in the family.

"But you do know her, Mum," he replied with a grin looking so smug that he had outsmarted everyone. "She's been in this house many times, and she's waiting for me to invite her in again."

He opened the back door and in walked Sandy. The look of both shock and relief on Heather's face was compelling. The whole family were ecstatic, even Stephen who was the first to get up and congratulate them along with Ruthann and Robin. Esther sat and smiled; she really didn't care but put on a brave face.

"You dark horse! How did you keep that a secret?" roared Robin.

"When's the big day?" asked Ruthann.

"As soon as we have the money, but it will be a quiet day, 'cause me and Sandy don't want any fuss."

Heather was overjoyed and trying to hold back her tears, thankful they were happy tears. "This is the best news I've heard in such a long time," she snivelled, "I couldn't have picked a better woman for you myself, Mosey. Joey would be so proud. How long has this been going on?"

"A good while, Mrs O'Donnell," said a shy but delighted Sandy.

"I can't believe it; I wondered why you were going over to Uncle John's a lot more Mosey. It's time this family had something to celebrate."

Ruthann excitedly butted in, "And Thomas can be your page-boy!"

It was out of her before she realised what she had said, turning to Esther for forgiveness, understanding how awful she must feel that Margot could have been flower girl, but Esther smiled at her forgivingly. Stephen caught this moment and quietly held her hand under the table, squeezing it tightly, but she rudely pushed him away, left the table and went over to Sandy.

"Welcome to the family, Sandy. I hope you and Mosey will be very happy. Can I see the ring?"

Mosey took the small box out of his pocket and opened it, to place a small sapphire ring on her finger while they all clapped.

"Oh, where is John?" inquired an impatient Heather. "I know he has champagne, and we need to celebrate. I'm so happy."

"I've seen to all that, Mum. He and Eileen are bringing it over."

Ruthann noticed Uncle John running across the road on his own. "He's coming now, but he's on his own and with no champagne?"

The back door was flung open and a troubled John declared loudly, "Have you heard the news?"

A look of panic crossed everyone's face. Heather shook her head in despair, not wanting anything to spoil this rare and wonderful occasion. "Oh no! What's happened, John?" she cried.

"There's been a car bomb at the Castle. It was the Commander's car, Esther!"

She jumped to her feet, screaming, "NO! NO! It can't be!"

"It's okay, he's okay Esther. He's in hospital, he's alright. It's that woman Stellabrass, she's dead! She got into the car and the bomb went off while he was coming out of the Castle, that's when it happened, it blew him off his feet, and he has minor injuries!"

Esther trembled, she didn't care anymore what anyone thought, she had to see him, and fast. "I need to see him. Bring me, Ruthann? I need to go now. I'm sorry, Mosey, I need to go! He needs me!"

Ruthann looked at Robin and Robin looked at Stephen. It was over. There was no point in him trying any longer. "Bring her, Ruthann," he said looking defeated.

Again, Heather saw the anguish on her daughter's face and how her body was shaking uncontrollably. When was all this going to end? She felt her pain and wanted to take some of it off her but knew she couldn't. Esther couldn't go on like this, something had to give. Maybe this was it.

They made enquiries and even though it was all highly confidential, Rueben had left orders that Esther McCarthy was to be told what happened and granted permission to see him if she wanted to. But of course, she wanted to! They found out he was in a Belfast Hospital and made their way there with very little conversation. Esther was in a state of trauma; the only thing she could think of was what if he had died? It was an unbearable thought, but it stirred something within her, and from here on, her life was going to be different. Ruthann noticed the beautiful diamond ring on her finger that had quickly replaced her gold wedding band, but she didn't ask any questions as it was obvious that Rueben had given it to her. Eventually, they arrived, and Esther jumped out.

"I'm coming with you!" Ruthann bellowed.

"Come on then. You can wait in the cafeteria."

They sprinted into the hospital having been given some directions secretly from Donny. Ruthann went to the small café at the front of the hospital while Esther ran on. Her destination was sealed off as if there was maintenance taking place. She panicked until she heard a voice call her.

"Esther!"

She turned to see Donny standing in civilian clothing, hardly recognising him. "Where is he, Donny?"

"Come on, I'll bring you. He knows you're coming."

She followed Donny down the long corridor through the sealed-off area and saw two military guards. As they went further, there were another two guards sitting at a doorway.

"That's the room," said Donny, pointing. "They've had their orders to let you through. Go quick."

Esther hurried down the corridor and into the room. There he was sitting up in bed in his pyjamas, waiting for her. His arm was in a sling, and he had a few scratches on his face. Beside him was one of the corporals sitting on a chair.

"You can leave now corporal!" he commanded. "And make sure the door stays closed. I want privacy!"

"Yes sir!" he replied and left the room closing the door.

Esther threw herself over him in turmoil, which amused him, and he gave a nervous laugh.

"Hey, you need to teach those nurses! This is the right way to treat a sick guy!"

But Esther didn't find his remark amusing. This was one of the most serious moments of her life, these next moments would determine their future. She couldn't speak for a few minutes, overcome with the sheer shock of it all, just stroked his face while he watched her contently then pulled her close to him.

"It's only scratches. I landed on my arm with the power of the blast. I'm okay," he said trying to reassure her, noticing the agony on her face.

She tried so hard to keep herself together but couldn't. "I don't know what I would have done if it had been you that was killed, Rueben. Life just wouldn't have been worth living. I couldn't go on. I mean that."

He was concerned by this and had every reason to be as he had things he needed to tell her, and she needed to be strong.

"Hey, you. I don't want to hear you talk like that. If anybody has a reason to live it's you. Look at Marianne, her life was taken from her so fast."

"I'm so sorry about Marianne. I feel so awful, all those nasty things I said to her."

He laughed at her reply, knowing how much they despised one another. "You certainly gave it to her big time."

"Will you miss her?" she asked.

He lifted her head and pulled her face over to him, kissing her. "Let's just say I'm very thankful it wasn't you."

He kissed her again, but Esther pulled back, this was serious, and she had something important to say. "I need you to listen to me, Rueben. I'm leaving Stephen, he knows, they all know. I'm going away with you. I've made my mind up. I'm never going to lose you again. I love you more than words can say and I'm not going to live another day without you in my life. That's it. No arguing. You and I are going to be together at last!"

She smiled a great happy smile, knowing she had unburdened a heavy weight that had been dragging her down for a long time. Her face was brighter now having confessed this decision, and anxiously waited for his approval, but there was nothing, no emotion, no excitement, no words, just a blank stare. She waited, her heart beating faster and faster until he put his hand on her face and stroked her. The joy changed to a sickly feeling, and her smile changed to terror, and the voice in her head cried No! No! Not again! She began weeping. He wiped the tears away. It was all too good to be true! Then he confirmed it.

"My darling, now I need you to listen to me very carefully. You have my ring on your finger. That will always be a reminder to you that you will never lose me. You have my heart; you've owned it from the first moment I laid eyes on you."

She couldn't hold the pain in any longer. "No, I don't want to hear this. It's too sore. Please don't, Rueben, you're killing me."

A tear rolled down his cheek, he didn't want to do this to her but there was no other way! They were both sore, yet he had to be in control to get through those moments so she could understand what he was saying was the right thing to do. It was vital that she did.

"Now, listen!" he seized her by her shoulders, shaking her head to look at him, as he spoke through her broken sobs, her face now soaked with tears trying as hard as she could to control her hysteria. "That bomb was meant for me. You know that, right?" She nodded her head. "Okay, I've been terminated from my post at Benbradagh and I have to be out of Northern Ireland first thing in the morning. There'll be a helicopter at 6 am, taking me somewhere, I don't know where right now. I don't have a say in this."

His words had an overpowering effect on Esther, freezing her whole body. It was a feeling of having no feeling, and it consumed her, but without realizing it, her body's reaction to trauma eased the pain that had now become normal. Her eyes watched his mouth as he relayed those words to her, those words she never wanted to hear.

"I won't be allowed back here, darling. Not for a very long time if ever. Now I need you to know that Marianne was only my business partner, she was never anything else. There was nothing going on between us, Esther, even though she wanted there to be. She did a few dirty deals, and I had to sort them out, in the process there were a few reprobate asses that were able to disclose that I wasn't just a Commander in the US Navy, as if that wasn't bad enough."

Esther looked at him like alarms had just gone off. "What do you mean you're not just a Commander? Who else are you?"

"I'm an undercover surveillance saboteur for the Israeli embassy."

She got up from the bed slowly and walked round to the other side. "What does that mean?"

"It means, my darling, I'm a spy! So, you see there's a lot I couldn't tell you. Right now, my life is in danger. I need you to believe me when I tell you I would have given all this up for you, but I can't now Esther. This hospital is surrounded by undercover police and military. They know everything about you, otherwise, you wouldn't have been allowed in to see me. Do you understand how serious this all is? That's the way my life is going to be. Do you want to live like that? You could only put up with it for a short while, I already feel smothered."

She put her head on his chest. "I don't care as long as I would be with you!"

He stroked her hair. "Life can be so damned cruel, my love. So damned cruel! You have no idea how strong and determined you are, Esther."

She sat up quickly looking confused. "Who are you really? I really don't know you at all. All I know is that who you really are, is taking you away from me. Do you understand?"

He looked at her deep in thought and found that to be profoundly true. He owed it to her to tell her everything he could. "I was born Benjamin Rueben Braunstein in Tiberius, Israel 1929. My family moved to Poland in 1935. My father was a hotelier, and my mother was a teacher for the Polish National Ballet."

Esther's eyes lit up. He was describing a completely different person to the one she knew. He went on, "I was to inherit the hotels, but in 1939 Hitler invaded Poland. They burned the hotels to the ground, and we fled. I don't know how, but I was separated from my parents and my sister Eliana while trying to get out of Poland. Unfortunately, I found out after the war that they were all murdered at Auschwitz in the concentration camps."

Esther was astounded. She couldn't believe what she was hearing. "I'm so sorry. So, what happened to you?"

She knew by the shiver in his voice he was trying not to break down. He swallowed and took a deep breath. "I ran for my life, then I met an American family living in Warsaw, they took me in and brought me up as one of their own. They gave me all the love and care I needed. Their name was Redpath. We moved to the States just after the war ended. I then went back to Israel to University and studied Law and Politics and back again back to the States. I met and married a lovely woman called Adele and we had a son together. The marriage didn't last, so we divorced, it was straight forward. I joined the forces and it pretty much all went from there. I worked my way to the top until Israeli intelligence approached me. I believed I could be of help, maybe I was, I really don't know. I speak four languages, English, Polish, Hebrew and Russian."

Esther shook her head. It was like she was just getting to know the man she had loved unquestioningly all these years. "So why? Why did you join Israeli Intelligence?"

"I felt I needed to do something that would stop atrocities like the extermination of the Jewish people during the war from ever happening again. I thought I could change the world. It didn't take long before I found out I couldn't. I couldn't stop the hurt and pain, I could only do what I'd been appointed in my life to do. Sometimes, my darling, you can know too much, and where there is much knowledge, there is much grief."

Esther wiped away a little tear that rolled down his face to his lips. "I didn't think it was possible to love you more, Rueben Redpath, but I do," she said passionately.

He smiled that big, beautiful smile that always made her feel special. "Let me hold you!" They held each other as tightly as they could for a few moments.

"So, tell me about Robert?"

He took a deep breath and looked out of the window. "Robert James Redpath joined the Navy, chip off the old block, you could say. He had just turned nineteen years old when he was killed in a road accident in Florida. He was on leave when it happened. He had only been buried a few months when I met you that November day sitting on the cowgate, remember, the day I lifted you in my arms and made love to you in the tent."

"How could I ever forget? I knew there was something different about you that day. Why didn't you tell me?"

"I guess I took it worse than I thought. It threw me right over the edge. That's why I couldn't contact you. I wanted to, but it was the lowest point of my life, and I couldn't do that to you. I finally got it together. I had only been back at Benbradagh one day when I saw you at your gate, I couldn't believe my luck, but it wasn't the time to tell you. Then, when you told me about your father and insisted that we couldn't see each other again, there just wasn't the right time."

She knew that was right, he never had the opportunity to tell her. They had always seized their time together like inhaling oxygen just to stay alive, just like they were doing now.

"Every time I look at you, Esther, I wonder what you ever saw in an old weasel like me. I never deserved you, but our times together have been so precious. I know you don't want to hear what I'm about to say but hear me out! I want you to go back home to your husband, he adores you and he will look after you. I can't do that for you now, I really wish I could. You have a family that loves you, you have a career, and you have a future!"

She cried, and so did he. "I can't let you go, Rueben. Please I can't go back to Stephen!" She grabbed hold of him like she was never letting go.

"Please, Esther! This is hard for both of us. You must be strong!" He raised her head once again to make her look at him and understand. Her face was red with emotional pain. "Listen to me, Esther. You must start allowing yourself to live again, my darling. You've got to. My stepmother once told me that when something within you dies, it makes way for a new birth, a new chapter. Seize it, Esther. The pain will go away when you understand the purpose."

She closed her eyes and put her arms right around him. "I'll never stop loving you! How can you let go of me?"

He pulled her by the hair to look at his face. "There's not a day that goes by that I'm not thankful for having you in my life. I'm not letting go of you, that's impossible, we have no choice but to move on in different directions. I have no damn control over this. Don't you understand?" He was starting to get irate, not with Esther but with the circumstances.

"I'll never understand, Rueben, but I know I have to, I can't walk out that door knowing I'm never going to see you again. I just can't! You also have to promise me something?"

He glared at her with hope in his eyes as if she could make the situation better, and in a way, she could. "Anything," he replied desperately.

She picked up a pen and note pad sitting on the cabinet beside his bed and wrote something down. Then stared at him strangely. "This may seem bizarrc but it's the only way I'm going to get through this." She handed him the piece of paper and he read it aloud,

"I'll meet you on the top of Benbradagh on the 7th of August 1995 at 3 pm." He smiled. "That's twenty years away, and it's our daughter's birthday."

"Is it a date?" she asked, nervous of his reply.

"If I'm still alive, Esther, I promise you darling I'll be there, nothing will stop me. I think it's a great idea. But what if…"

She put her hand over his mouth. "No what if's, Rueben."

His face lightened. "Here's to twenty years' time. May we both be alive and well, and let's hope the damn war here will have ended!"

They seized their last few moments together, only allowing their eyes to do the talking and held hands. Then Esther got off the bed and walked slowly to the door. He called to her, her heart breaking like never before.

"I'll get them to fly past your house in the morning. Will you be there?"

"Of course, I'll be there! I'll always love you! Thank you for loving me," and she left.

He replied, "dopoki znow sie nie spotkamy, kochanie." (Polish for "Until we meet again, my darling.")

Nineteen

She didn't sleep that night; all she could do was cry believing she may never see him again. Heather heard her cries knowing there was nothing she could do. Esther just wept. Never again would he drive past in his jeep, sit in Renny's with a brandy, or entertain at the Castle. From now on, it would only be memories. How could she ever be happy again?

At 5.30 am, Esther paced up and down outside the cottage, grief-stricken. This would be the final time she'd get to see him or at least a glimpse of him. Today would not be a good day to make any decisions on how to move forward and make her life work again, not when she felt it would be so much easier just to die with a broken heart. It was like a large part of her body had been mutilated and nothing could ever replace it. She strolled along the road to the cowgate and leaned over it, weeping. If she only had known all those years ago what was going to happen that first day she set eyes on him, she would have made a run for it, then laughed through the tears knowing full well that wouldn't have been the case. She recalled the strange feeling she felt when she met him; was it all meant to be?

Her reminiscing was interrupted by a whirring sound hovering in the distance. She leapt up quickly and there was the helicopter flying towards her. She dashed further up the road to meet it, raising her arms and shouting, "I love you, Rueben Redpath!"

It flew down as low as it could, and she could just about see him waving. It swirled about for a few moments, and she laughed at the madness of it all, but then it began to fly higher and higher into the distance and the laughter turned into more tears.

"I'll see you in 1995. Please stay alive, my darling. Please."

The helicopter had gone completely and there wasn't a sound. All was quiet, just the cows mooing in the field and the sound of the wind through the trees. It was over. There was a weird feeling of closure that gave her the tiniest amount of peace. She looked up to Benbradagh, knowing that it was never going to be the same again, nothing would be. Again, she had to go through the grieving process. Could she do this? Would she see him in twenty years' time? She had that feeling of Yes!

As she walked back down to the cottage, the rain came on really quickly and very heavily. She got soaked but she didn't care; it actually seemed to help the pain. In the distance, she spied Mosey putting on his overalls in the yard. He saw her, then he did something very unlike him. He strode briskly up to meet her. Without a word, he wrapped his coat around her, holding her tight and walked back to the cottage in the pouring rain, while she rested her head on his shoulder wailing hysterically. Her mother watching at the window, cried too. She opened the back door and took over from Mosey holding her until she got her to settle down on the chair at the window.

"I'll make a cup of tea for us, love."

Placing the cups down in front of them, she said, "I'm so sorry, Esther, I really mean that, love. I wish you could have gone with him. I know how much you love each other. I didn't always, but I do now."

"This stupid bloody country!" cried Esther.

The next day, Stephen and Esther had a very long talk. They did get back together, and he built her that beautiful house in the field with the veranda, and together they lived in it for many happy years. Esther went back to school and got a degree in Journalism; she also became a mother of twin boys, Stephen Junior and John-Joe and they grew up to be like their dad in many ways, kind-hearted and strong. Stephen doted on them. Mosey and Sandy also got married and lived at the cottage with Heather. It wasn't long before a whole new generation had taken over the O'Donnell cottage as they had three children one after the other, Shay, Laverne and Daniel. There were lots of happy family years with children's parties, birthdays and Christmases. It all seemed so normal. John finally married Eileen, and she moved in with him at the big house. They loved the kids and were grandparents to them all. Ruthann unfortunately had health problems and after having an urgent hysterectomy, was unable to have any more children; it was now Esther's turn to be her confidante and help while she was going through this ordeal, but eventually, she came to terms with it, very grateful to be alive.

Heather quietly sat back and watched her family grow. There wasn't a day that went by when she didn't think how much Joey would have loved all his grandchildren, and she could see Mosey's two boys very like him in ways; Shay even inheriting the dimple on the chin.

Esther had many joyful times being a wife and mother, but as the boys grew into teenagers, her career began to flourish, and she found herself spending more of her time in Belfast where she worked presenting an afternoon magazine programme for Ulster Television. She had seen Rueben a few times on the international news in the run-up to the Presidential elections when George H. W. Bush took over office from Ronald Reagan. He was also interviewed on political talk shows after the collapse of the Soviet Union in 1991. How proud she was of him. He looked older, but his new grey highlights just emphasized those deep brown eyes she knew so well. Now, even more than ever he was in her thoughts.

The inevitable happened in 1992 when Stephen and Esther divorced. It was a clean-cut split without courts or any bitterness. The boys stayed with their father while Esther moved to a modern apartment in Belfast, but she would come up and stay every weekend spending quality time with all the family. It was like she had paid in full for everything she owed to Stephen, and more, and now they could part, mutually understanding that both parties had given their all to the marriage. The twins had now turned seventeen and were naturally sad to see their parents part, but Esther was truthful to them about Rueben and Margot, and they visited her grave often.

Esther never told anyone about her prearranged date with Rueben in 1995 and as that day grew closer, she could feel herself as excited as she was all those years ago. Nothing would stop this reunion, or could it? The 7th of August fell on a Monday, and it worked out well as Stephen and the boys were going camping for the weekend and wouldn't be back until that night. Stephen's now year-long girlfriend, Linda, was also joining them. Esther found Linda to be everything that Stephen needed, and it was plain to see she was madly in love with him. She stayed at the cottage as Mosey and Sandy always made her very welcome, and she loved spending time with them.

It was now Saturday the 5th of August 1995 and Mosey made a last-minute decision that he and Sandy would take the kids camping with Stephen up at the North Coast. The kids were so excited. Esther thought this would be a good opportunity to take Heather to see Ruthann in Limavady and they could go shopping. It was a lovely day, so they stopped off and had lunch in a characterful little pub just outside the town. Heather noticed Esther to be particularly quiet and wasn't sure if it was because Ruthann, after having a glass or two of the house wine, talked endlessly about Thomas receiving his degree in Photography, or if there was something wrong. Esther dropped Ruthann off, and she and Heather headed back to the cottage. They were both tired and went to bed early. Their Sunday was spent going to church, cleaning around the graves and cooking a roast dinner together. Heather was still suspicious of Esther's overly quiet behaviour.

The next morning, Esther woke with her heart beating like a drum. This was the day she had spent the last 20 years waiting for and found herself wrestling with the thought of him not turning up, but she knew he hadn't died so he had to be there, if he hadn't met someone else that is, but he promised! This was torment, but the sound of her mother getting up at 8 am released her. Heather had a lie-in as eight in the morning was late for her, but the house was quiet, and Esther reckoned she was probably taking advantage of the peace and quiet. She joined her for breakfast, nervous and excited but trying not to show it. She couldn't eat, only having a cup of coffee.

"What's wrong with you, Esther?" Heather asked giving her that look as if she was a child again.

"What do you mean? Nothing is wrong with me," she replied surprised that even at her age her mother could still fathom her out.

"Come on Esther, I'm your mother. I know there's something not right. Is it Rueben?"

"What?" Esther was staggered at her guess; his name hadn't been mentioned in years and yet, today of all days, she must have picked up on something.

"I can see that look in your eye," she added.

Esther didn't answer which made Heather even more cagey. "I remember that look from years back when you started seeing him. I haven't seen it again, until now. I'm your mother, I know you. You don't have to hide this from me now. You've heard from him, haven't you?"

Esther was completely bowled over. She was a mother herself but could never be as perceptive as Heather. She smiled and gave in, happy that now she was free to talk about him without all the guilt and agony.

"No, Mum. I haven't heard from him," she said, smiling.

Heather stared at her peculiarly and asked, "What's going on then?"

"I'm meeting him later today at the top of Benbradagh."

Heather's face lit up and then a little tear rolled down her cheek. "How did this happen?"

Esther explained to her the last conversation they had and the plan they made for that day.

"And it's Margot's birthday too. What a perfect day for it. He'll be there, Esther, I just know it. It's your time love and I'm so happy for you."

If only Heather knew how important those words were to her right now. "Thank, you Mum."

Heather reached over the table and took her by the hand. It was one of those moments Esther would never forget. She watched as the tears fell from her eyes and waited earnestly for her next sentence.

"Grab this chance of happiness, love. You deserve it. I know how lonely life can be! I watched everything you went through, and you went through it with dignity. All those years you tried hard to make your marriage work, and you did for a while, but your heart was always with Rueben. I want you to know how proud I am of you, love. No more hiding. No more trying to please others."

Never had there been a time in her life when she had seen her mother so unassuming and frank. Esther lifted Heather's hand and kissed it. "You're the best mum a girl could ever have!" and Heather smiled.

"Now go and make yourself beautiful for him, Esther, just like your namesake did in the bible. It's your time to shine!"

Esther spent the rest of the morning preparing to meet Rueben. She had carefully planned everything, from what she was wearing to what they would talk about. Shaking with excitement, but then came those negative thoughts. What if he's forgotten all about today, as he's always so busy? The thoughts began to torment her again until she felt sick. It was time to go and get the questions answered. Heather hugged her as she went out to the car.

"You look beautiful, Esther!"

She was now in her late forties but still as beautiful as all those years ago, only a lot wiser. Casually but thoughtfully, she wore her new jeans with a loose white blouse and comfy navy kickers. She pulled her hair back in a sleek ponytail and threw her navy V-neck jumper over her shoulders, then last but not least, her infamous dark sunglasses. Now she was on her way! Heather had noticed the diamond ring on her finger but never mentioned it. She watched Esther from the window as the car spiralled up the mountain, wishing she had Joey there to talk to him about this long-running love story that now, at long last, his daughter could unashamedly pursue.

Twenty

Esther parked her car at the summit. There was no one around. It looked as if part of the walkway was closed off, but that wasn't going to stop her, nothing was going to get in the way of this meeting, not even yellow tape and signposts. She walked to the old naval base that was now just the foundations of what had been there all those years ago. It had now become a tourist attraction with parents bringing their children and teaching them about the Cold War and how Benbradagh played a massive part, in communicating with the American naval vessels out on the North Atlantic. She walked around, thankful it was a fine day, with just a little breeze and only a few clouds. Her heart was beating so fast she thought it was going to jump out of her body, never had she felt so nervous, not even undertaking her first live TV programme made her feel this anxious.

It was three o'clock. She looked right around in a 360-degree turn while circling his ring on her finger. She looked at her watch again, it was two minutes past three. He wasn't coming, there was no sign of any cars or trucks, nothing! This was all too much, twenty years had gone by, and he had probably forgotten all about it. Then suddenly there was a noise in the distance, she recognised it. It was the sound of a helicopter, that same sound when she waved goodbye to Rueben all those years ago. Of course, he would come in a helicopter, that made sense now.

She looked up and it was getting closer. She froze to the spot knowing it was him but quickly renewed her strength when the helicopter landed, and she ran to it. The door opened slowly and she stopped immediately when two men jumped out, and for one awful moment, she thought he had sent a messenger to tell her he wasn't coming, until they pulled steps down and there he was, the man who had given her more heartache than she deserved, the Commander she had fallen in love with over twenty-five years ago and never stopped loving. He was just as handsome; the years had been kind to him. She ran to him with tears, but this time tears of joy.

"Rueben! Rueben!" she cried out.

He watched as she hurtled towards him, opening his arms wide and shouted, "Esther! My beautiful Esther! You're still that beautiful girl I met all those years ago!"

They threw their arms around each other. She could smell that very same beautiful aftershave that he always wore. She kissed him and he held her so tightly. It took a few minutes before they could let go of one another, then he took her by the hand and they walked, but as they did, Esther noticed he was using a walking stick. They didn't speak, they just walked as he seemed to know where he was going, and they could have walked to Timbuktu for all she cared as long as he had her by the hand. It then dawned on her where they were going. There it was, the tent with two chairs and a table outside it, but with a bottle of brandy and two brandy glasses.

"Come with me, my beauty!" He pulled the chair out for her, and she sat down. "We never did have that brandy, did we? We were always being interrupted, but there'll be no interruptions today. And you still have the God-damned war going on here!"

She laughed as cheerfully, as he poured out a little brandy in both glasses and handed her one. "Slainte!" they both said together, raising their glasses. She already had that fuzzy feeling, but the warmth of the brandy relaxed her right to the core. This was like a dream. This important day she had waited for all these years was now here and all the stuff that had kept them apart had gone, finished!

"How are you, Esther? Has life been kind?"

And that was it, they talked about everything and laughed. It was wonderful.

"How did you manage to do all this, Rueben?" she asked, pointing to the tent, table and chairs.

"You know, I have my ways and means. It hasn't changed, they still do what I tell them. Did you think we were just going to arrive and have people standing about watching us?"

"So, you got the place cordoned off!" She laughed as he reminded her how influential he was.

He knew everything about Esther, from her boys to her career and commended her on being so strong and getting on with her life. They talked about Stephen and his new life.

"But what about you, Esther? Surely, you've had your admirers?"

"I have had admirers, Rueben, but I could never forget you or stop loving you. Never! What about you, did you ever meet anyone, special?" she asked nervously.

"Yes, I did!" he replied. She could feel that pain tugging at her, and she watched him as he took a sip of brandy and then, setting the glass back down on the table, he looked her straight in the eye, "But that was over twenty-five years ago, and I met her just at the bottom of this mountain!"

He got up and walked to the exact spot where she remembered how strange he had seemed all those years ago. She noticed him again staring out at the landscape in that same way.

"Remember that night in Renny's?" he said. "It seems like an age away now. I knew I could never love anyone but you," then he turned and asked, "How are Tommy and Rita? Do they still have our room?"

She giggled remembering how nosey Rita was. "The room is still there, and Tommy and Rita are still there. They often talked about the big Yankee official that would come and stay with them."

He laughed at the thought and limped back over to the chair. She noticed how reliant he was on the stick, and thought he must have hurt himself. He sat down and held her hand.

"From one breathtaking view to another," he said as he stared at her like she was the only other human being in the world. She stroked his face and there was silence. "I love you so much, Esther."

"I love you too, Rueben," she said letting go of his hand and taking a handkerchief out of her pocket and handing it to him. "That belongs to you!"

He looked puzzled. "Me?"

"That's the handkerchief you handed me in Renny's the day I got soaked in the rain. You were sitting at the fire sipping brandy, remember? I've kept it ever since. It helped me get through the tough days."

"Oh Esther, my darling Esther, I'm so sorry I had to leave you."

He closed his eyes and gritted his teeth for a second as if he was in pain, but then he smiled as if he was embarrassed, and took her by the arm. "Let's have another brandy. We'll drink to Margot, Robert and Joey."

They clinked glasses, remembering all the hurt and pain they both endured, until Esther asked that all-important question, "What happened to your leg, Rueben?"

He shook his head hesitating to answer. "There's no easy way to say this, so I'm just going to tell it as it is. I have cancer. They said if I look after myself properly and take the medication, I could have six months or so."

He watched sadly as her face turned from joy to sorrow. This was the last thing he had wanted to tell her, he just wanted to leave while she was happy, go home and quietly die alone in New York, that was his plan, but as they sat together, he knew he couldn't lie to her. Esther jumped up from the table and went slowly to Rueben's spot. It was her turn to stare across the landscape. She couldn't believe what he had just said, it all seemed so unfair. All these years she'd waited for this day, hoping for that happy ever-after ending. Why? She had so much rage within her!

"What have I ever done so bad in my life to deserve this!" she cried, not recognising how insensitive that statement was. She held her stomach and bowed her head crying so hard, as Rueben watched helplessly. She fell to the ground as if it was the final blow. She lay for a few moments crying, and then curiously arose and danced over to him like something intriguingly spiritual had taken place. "Right, Rueben, from here on in, right to the last day of your life, we are not going to be parted. I don't want to hear any arguments or excuses because that's the way it is!"

He put his finger to her mouth, shushing her to be quiet. She looked fearful. "Listen to me, Esther. Just answer me this question." She looked even more horrified now. Could her body stand anymore? She glared at him while he had the impertinence to laugh, then he said. "It's a question I asked you in this same spot many years ago. Will you marry me?"

She let out a gasp of relief, then cried out so loudly, "Yes! Yes! Yes!" and began jumping up and down, raising her arms in the air.

Amused by her response, he went over and pulled her close to him. She melted in his arms, just like that girl whose heart he stole all those years ago, as he kissed her and asked, "Will you dance with me, Esther?"

She replied, "I would love to dance with you, Rueben."

And he sang The Last Waltz, the song they danced to that special night at Rennys, and now they waltzed together on top of Benbradagh mountain.

That was that. Esther packed her bags and went off with Rueben. Their first stop was Arkansas, where they got married, with Katrina and Ralph as witnesses. It was the most beautiful day of their lives, not even the dark shadow of cancer could ruin it. The next stop was Rueben's New York apartment. They made wonderful memories together, sightseeing all the famous landmarks, eating at beautiful restaurants and watching people at their designated summer seat in the park with a flask of coffee. Esther stayed by his side every moment. The last two weeks of his life were so difficult as Rueben deteriorated quickly but died peacefully holding Esther's hand. At his request, she organised a quiet burial at the Jewish graveyard in New

York. Heather flew over with Stephen Jr and John-Joe to be with her at that tragic time. It was all over.

When she arrived back home, Esther went to Benbradagh and lay a dozen red roses at the spot where Rueben had stood many times.

She never returned there again.

Available worldwide from Amazon
and all good bookstores

www.mtp.agency

mtp.agency

@mtp_agency

Printed in Great Britain
by Amazon